DREAMING OF HER

DREAMING OF HER

by

Maggie Morton

2012

This Trade Paperback Original Is Published By
Bold Strokes Books, Inc.
P.O. Box 249
Valley Falls, NY 12185

First Edition: September 2012

Credits
Editor: Shelley Thrasher
Production Design: Susan Ramundo
Cover Design By Sheri (graphicartist2020@hotmail.com)

Acknowledgments

I'd like to begin by thanking Len Barot for accepting my novel and letting me join the Bold Strokes Books lovely crew of writers. I would also like to thank the immensely helpful people from BSB who have been ever so supportive, as well as willing to answer all of my questions (and there were a lot!). These people include Kim Baldwin, Cindy Cresap, Connie Ward, and Sandy Lowe. I'd especially like to thank my terrific, intelligent, and far-beyond-competent editor, Shelley Thrasher. I was incredibly lucky to wind up with an editor who "got" me as an author, one who was clearly interested in strengthening my writing and skills as a writer. I'd also like to thank my first, unofficial, editor, who gave me a very large amount of help in getting the novel to a point where it was actually possible it would get accepted and published. And lastly, I'd like to thank my number one fan, Bucko, who believed in me all along, and always has—being with him is like a dream come true.

Dedication

To Bucko, the man of my dreams

CHAPTER ONE

Isa raised her hand to the knocker, then hesitated. She was nervous about this night, even though she was pretty certain she looked amazing. She wore a skin-tight burgundy dress, with her eyes lined in black, her lips painted red, and her hair styled in a messy look that said, "I've just been fucked, and I don't care if you know." And who knew, maybe she'd get a chance to say that to someone inside. After all, she was meeting someone here, someone who certainly hadn't been subtle about what she would do to Isa.

But would she allow this woman to touch her, to even come close to her? She was uncertain—she just hadn't decided quite yet. Partially, maybe even entirely, it was because she'd never been with a woman before, and she didn't even know what this woman looked like, just that she'd be here, waiting for her, and that this woman wanted her, wanted her desperately. But would Isa…would she decide to locate this woman? And if she did, would she do the things this woman had suggested? Dirty things that required undressing, touching, kissing…and more?

Well, she had to admit she was curious enough to be willing to enter the mansion, so she raised her hand to the silver knocker, knocked twice, then waited. It only took a few moments for someone to answer—a man who looked like he might be a servant, who wore a tuxedo. She was surprised that anyone here was wearing clothes, but perhaps the servants were excluded from the fun. From the fucking, to be precise.

"Enter, miss, if you please." He opened the door wide, and then there was no turning back. Isa took one step into the house, and then another, and after a few more she heard the quiet sound of the door being shut behind her.

It took her a few moments to get used to the low light in the place, and then, as her eyes adjusted, she began to take in the room that spread out shortly after the hallway she stood in. The room was full of people, all wearing black satin masks, all in various states of undress. And the ones who were the most undressed were locked in congress, either getting ready to fuck or right in the middle of fucking. She couldn't help getting incredibly turned on in mere moments, just from the sight. Something (possibly her pussy) pulled her forward, and she was inside the room only seconds later. Once there, she scanned the room, leaping from body to body, from flesh to flesh.

Her body was reacting in hard-to-miss ways, amidst all this nudity, all this incredibly hot depravity. A completely naked man approached her, his interest impossibly clear, as his dick was pointing straight toward her like a divining rod. "Are you free right now?" he asked, a bold smile joining his words.

"No, I'm…meeting someone here."

"Oh, you are? Who?"

"Her name is…" And then she realized she didn't know her name. What was she doing at a sex party, meeting someone—a woman—whose name she didn't even know?

"Ah, I think I know who. She's up the stairs." He gestured beyond all the people that lay and stood in front of them, and she saw a wide staircase at the other side of the room, with lacquered black banisters and ruby-colored carpeted steps.

"Is this her house?" she asked him, but he was already gone, most likely searching for someone to fill his needs in place of her.

She threaded her way through the people, stepping over a few legs and torsos, her arms brushing against a few very intimate body parts—a hard cock and a woman's bush—but when their owners looked at her, she just shook her head. She had a mission—she was here for her, and her alone, and, she realized now, absolutely no one else would do.

She soon arrived at the bottom of the stairs and got ready to climb them, but first she took off her heels. The velvet carpet on the stairs, incredibly sensuous against her bare feet, caressed the sole of each foot.

At the top of the stairs was a set of double doors, but this time she didn't knock. The woman knew she was coming, and she knew the woman wanted her here. She slowly opened the door on the right side and entered the room, then turned and pushed the door shut.

"You're here," came a voice, sexy and rather deep, but clearly a woman's.

And there she lay, on the bed, completely naked, and Isa almost shook from pure, undiluted need.

"Yes, I'm here."

Isa took her in. The woman had thick, garnet-colored hair that hung down to her nipples, almost obscuring them, but luckily for Isa, not quite. And then her curves. Oh, someone could talk about them for days—a true hourglass figure, unlike Isa's own more subtle curves. But instead of being jealous of her perfect beauty, she just drank this gorgeous woman in, taking in her face last, which was the cherry on top of the sundae, with lips as pink as her cheeks and eyes a most startling gold.

The woman smiled and said simply, "Undress."

Who on earth could turn down a woman like her? And so off came her dress, messing up her dark, curly hair a little, then her panties. Now she was naked and all of her belonged to the woman on the bed. Most of her nerves had fled by then, but they were still there, just a little, and as she climbed onto the large, four-poster bed, she couldn't help but notice her body's slight tension. The woman noticed it too.

"Are you nervous, my darling? Those wide-open, lovely gray eyes of yours seem to say you are." She cupped Isa's chin. "You have nothing to worry about. I know it's your first time, and you don't have to do anything you don't want to."

"There isn't *anything* I don't want to do," she said, and she meant it more than she wanted to admit.

"Good. Well, I know a tried and true way to get rid of all those nasty little trickles of nervousness. Although, very occasionally, it can cause more. Tell me—have you ever eaten pussy?"

"No, never. You want me to do that to you?" Isa bit her lower lip, breaking eye contact for a moment, but her eyes were soon back on the woman's lovely face.

"Yes, I do, very much. I can already tell you'll find it as easy as riding a bicycle." The woman lay back on the plush array of pillows and spread her legs, revealing the first pussy Isa had ever come face to face with. It was surprisingly beautiful, with full, flushed lips and what must have been her clit, standing at attention right above a very appealing hole, one that she couldn't help but begin to tease with her fingers. The woman sighed, softly, and so she eased a finger, then two, inside her. It was warm, wet, even wonderful in there, and, well, she just *had* to taste her. So she dove right in.

Although Isa really had no idea what to do, it still seemed like she was doing well enough, considering the sounds the woman was making, sounds that pleased her to the bone, sounds that made her just as wet as the pussy pressed up against her tongue. Sounds that almost made Isa come just from their vibrations. And then, moments later, the woman was coming, screaming in ecstasy, making it clear that she had this down, that she had gotten it down fast.

She pulled back then, gazing up at the face above her, a face that held a delighted grin and glinting, golden eyes "Did you enjoy yourself, my darling?"

"Yes, oh yes, of course. Is it…could you…" She raised herself up onto her knees. Hopefully, if she was very, very lucky, the favor would be returned.

"If you want, I will—beep beep beep beep."

"Huh?" *What on earth did that mean?*

"Beep beep beep…"

Isa's eyes slowly slid open. *Fuck.* Her alarm was going off, and her boyfriend was already reaching over her to turn it off. He looked hot—although not as hot as her dream woman—but before she could suggest anything, perhaps a quick screw to make up for her dream being interrupted, he leapt out of bed.

"I'm gonna go take a quick shower," he said.

"Do you think we could have sex first, sweetie?" She arranged her body in as alluring a posture as possible, letting the sheets slip down to reveal her low-cut silk nightgown.

"Sorry, but I really need to get clean. Man, you sure were making weird noises in your sleep. Were you having a nightmare?"

Not bothering to wait for an answer, he stripped off his boxers and tossed them on the floor by the bathroom door, revealing the gym-toned body that wasn't hers to enjoy, at least right now.

"Damn it," she said softly, as the bathroom door shut behind him. Then the shower came on, and moments later Martin was singing, loudly and off-key, like he always did.

Well, it would be up to her trusty pocket rocket, as usual. Lately, it seemed he never wanted to have sex. *Weren't men supposed to always be up for it?* Maybe the dream was telling her something, maybe that she needed to give women a try.

Thoughts of dumping him had already been dancing through her head. Not as sweet as sugarplums, but the thoughts were becoming surprisingly appealing. Their lack of a sex life lately wasn't the only problem in their relationship, at least in her eyes. The romance was gone, replaced by fighting, and Martin had put quite a bit of distance between them.

But these thoughts weren't exactly a turn-on, and an orgasm—or two—needed to happen, and fast. Pushing those thoughts out of her mind, she clicked on her trusty vibe and pulled down her panties.

CHAPTER TWO

Downstairs, Isa took in the lovely weather. Spring at last. She said hello to her neighbor, who was sitting on the bench in front of their apartment building reading a romance novel, which was pretty much the only thing she had ever seen her elderly neighbor do. This one had the usual overly muscular guy on the cover, and this particular swarthy hottie happened to be a pirate, with a woman draped over his arm, probably melting from the passion that poured from each and every one of his pores.

"Hello, my dear," her neighbor said. She was pushing seventy at the very least, but Isa was always happy to see her as not at all ready to throw in the towel where passion was involved. Neither was she herself, she realized. But as delightful as her neighbor was, Isa really didn't want to know if she and her husband still went at it like rabbits.

Her neighbor placed a bookmark inside the book and smiled at her. "Off to Vivian's, are we? Time to write some more…blog posts, is it?"

"Yep, that's the plan."

"Well, tell her I say hello, if she's working today. Such a lovely woman. I really hope she can find a good man someday. Maybe I should set her up with one of my son's younger friends."

Isa held back the fact that Vivian didn't need to find a man, but a woman. "Well, I don't think setting people up usually works," she said. Hopefully that would be enough to keep her neighbor's matchmaking plans at bay. "I'm off, then. Enjoy your book."

"Oh, I will. It's just getting good, too." And the only word to describe the look on her neighbor's face at that moment was "lecherous." Isa grinned as she walked away. Hopefully she'd still be raring to go at seventy, too.

The walk to Vivian's was a short one, but she still took her time, enjoying the spring flowers popping up in her neighbors' small gardens and the wisteria draped over the tall gate of one house. The neighborhood she lived in with Martin was certainly nice, but she could only just afford it with what she earned from her blogging and the occasional fluff article on the side. Of course, one of the ongoing problems in their relationship was Martin's lack of contribution to the household expenses. He'd lost his job a number of months ago, and admittedly, it was a hard time to find work, but she really wished he'd been putting more effort into looking for a new job. A *lot* more effort, as he wasn't really looking at all, nor had he in the past. He certainly wasn't under-qualified—with a degree in architecture from a top school—but the mid-sized company he'd been working for had closed due to mismanagement.

The day was too beautiful for her to worry about things she had no control over, though, so she shoved all these relationship-based concerns out of her head and pushed open the door to Vivian's instead. Time to enjoy a croissant, one of Vivian's amazing mochas, and to do as much writing as she could.

Luckily for her, today Vivian was behind the counter, her short dreadlocks mostly covered by a pink, paisley handkerchief. As usual, her face was free of makeup, but she was so beautiful she had absolutely no need for it.

"Hello, darling," Vivian said, bringing to mind another woman using the same pet name for her. She tried to fight off the oncoming flush starting to paint her cheeks, but it was hopeless.

Vivian chuckled. "What's gotten you all rosy-cheeked? Have a good morning?" Vivian wiggled her eyebrows at her, only succeeding at furthering Isa's embarrassment.

"Something like that. Any chance we could change the subject?"

"Sure, sure. Hey, you hear back on that story you submitted yet?"

Isa had tried her hand yet again at writing fiction, but she was still having absolutely no luck getting her stories published. "Maybe I'm really meant for non-fiction, you know?"

"So, no luck with that one. Sorry to hear it. Well, then, what would you like today?"

"I'd like a croissant and a mocha, no whipped cream, one percent milk, please."

"Your usual, then? And a croissant? Must be a rough morning. Maybe you can tell me about it. It's been slow this last half hour, past the morning rush and before the lunch rush."

"Sounds great to me. I have a lot on my mind. Stupid relationship stuff, actually."

"Martin, eh? Well, we'll talk soon." Vivian got to work on her drink order, but first she had removed a delicious-looking croissant from the pastry case. It took a second for her to notice that Vivian had placed it on a different plate than usual—eye-catching and garnet-colored. Another reminder of her dream. Well, apparently whoever controlled these things wasn't going to let her forget about it. Probably all day long, at least with her luck, reminders would pop up everywhere. Not that the dream was that easy to forget in the first place.

She thought about it in more detail now, about its pure vividness—the beauty of the woman's face, the taste of her pussy, both of them so very lovely, and soon she was almost back there, touching the woman's body, tasting her, and waiting desperately for her own turn.

Then Vivian appeared back in front of her, shocking her back to the real world with the *clunk* of the mug hitting the counter. "That'll be six fifty-eight, hon."

"Yeah, just a second." She reached into her bag and took out her wallet, giving Vivian eight dollars. "Put the rest in the tip jar, okay?"

"Thanks. Enjoy." Vivian nodded at her and she picked up her order, taking it over to the window seats and settling into one of the high, black-cushioned stools. *Time to get to work.* Well, almost time, as she watched Vivian leave the counter and head to the next stool over.

Vivian peeled off a small piece of her croissant and popped it into her mouth. "Payment for hearing your tales of relationship woe...because, after all, at least you're in one." Vivian grinned at her, then nodded and said, "Well? You two still going to be together by day's end?"

"I really don't know. I mean...no? Maybe? I've been with him so long, my longest relationship to date, actually, so...I... well, at the very least, we need to have a talk. About how he's been acting, and the fact that he hasn't been looking for a job, or even pitching in with the housework."

"But you've got to realize, none of that's new. You've been talking about all this for weeks, and I don't see the scruffy, snarling tiger changing his stripes any time soon. Reminds me of *my* last relationship, which was sometime in the Paleolithic Era, I think."

"It hasn't been *that* long, has it? I mean, it was at least the Mesolithic."

"Very funny, jerk. At least I'm not in a dead-end relationship I'm not smart enough to get out of."

"Touché. And you do kind of have a point there, I guess." She took a sip of her mocha. "So, you really think I should end it? After so long together, it seems like such a waste."

"No, a waste is staying with someone who's a rude dickface when you could be with someone great. *That's* a waste. Look up the word 'waste.' It'll be an entry in the dictionary with Martin's face next to it."

"You might be right. I'll think it over while I work. Speaking of which, I need to get started. Thanks for the talk, Vivian."

"Any time, hon."

Now it was time to start writing. On the docket for today was a minimum of twelve entries for the women-oriented blog she wrote for, "Ladies First." It was a mixture of feminism, politics, and makeup. She turned to her computer screen and didn't look up from said screen until a little under four hours (and eleven entries) later. But when she took in the view outside the window with her now-tired eyes, she saw her friend Patricia dashing down the opposite side of the street. She waved, but Patricia didn't notice, in too much of a rush to notice anything, it seemed.

They hadn't made any plans to meet up that day, so she figured Patricia was swinging by for a surprise visit. Well, it was an okay time for her to take a break, so she typed the last few sentences of a post she would edit in a bit, then packed up her stuff and got ready to go. "I just saw my friend running down the street," she told Vivian, "so I should probably head home to meet her."

"Okay, Isa, you take care."

The weather had worsened while she had been writing, and now it was cold and cloudy. She paused outside the door for a second and felt something strange, almost like she wasn't supposed to go back to her apartment. Yep, that was strange, all right. And crazy. She hadn't seen Patricia in ages. It seemed like she was always busy when Isa wanted to get together with her, so it would really be nice to see her again. She crossed the street and started heading for her place, having to fight the wind as she walked. She certainly wasn't dressed for this weather and cursed softly as it began to sprinkle. Her laptop bag might have been waterproof, but her shorts and tank top certainly weren't, and as the rain started coming down faster, she sped up.

The front door of her building was slightly ajar when she arrived, and a small puddle of water was forming on the tile inside. She paused to shut it before she headed toward the stairs. If Patricia had been the last one to open it, she must have been in a hurry to get upstairs. But why would that be?

As she walked up the stairs to the floor their place was on, she heard sounds of muffled fighting coming from somewhere in the building. And as it turned out, they were coming from her apartment. A little hesitant, but certainly curious, she unlocked the door and slowly opened it. No one was in the living room, but obviously Martin and Patricia were there. After all, Patricia was doing most of the yelling.

"It's either her or me, Martin. You *know* this. So fucking grow a pair and choose."

Then Martin spoke, his voice much quieter, a touch of fear clear in his tone. "But she'll kick me out, sweetie. It's only her name on the lease, and she's been paying rent for the past three months. There's no way I'll be able to find a new place, especially one I can afford."

Before Patricia could reply, Isa turned the corner and entered the kitchen, and there they stood, Martin and Patricia, with her arms raised and an incredibly angry expression. Then, once Martin noticed her standing there, she saw him look more surprised than she'd ever seen him. He even gasped.

"You fucker. *Both* of you. How…how could you? And with Patricia?" She turned to her friend, and guessed Patricia could easily see that her own fury certainly went beyond even hers.

"And you, Patricia? All these months, all this time you've been 'busy,' or whatever? You know what? Fuck you!" She pointed at Martin. "You—get out. You can pick up your stuff later. Just fucking get out!"

Martin froze, appearing terrified, and then he and Patricia left the room, Martin practically running out of the apartment. But after he'd exited through the front door Isa had slammed open, Patricia paused, her face full of something like regret. But it was a little too late for that. "I'm…sorry, Isa. I'm so sorry." And it was also too late for apologies.

"Okay." That was all she could say.

Once Patricia had left, she shut and locked the door, then she wandered into the kitchen. What were you supposed to do when you learned your boyfriend had been cheating on you with a very close friend? She didn't know, so she leaned against the counter for a bit and pondered the situation.

Finally an idea struck. She got out some brownie mix and turned on the oven. About an hour later, half a pan of brownies sat in her lap, barely cool enough to eat. The other half had burned her tongue effectively, but what was a little pain when anger and mild heartbreak were there, too?

CHAPTER THREE

Lilith might have stepped back through her mirror into her village hours ago, but she was still thinking of the woman whose dream she'd last been in. The woman had been beautiful, of course, because although it was rather against the rules for her and her fellow Dreammakers—the ones who created and controlled sex dreams for their particular human city—Lilith didn't bother to interact with any woman even slightly less than gorgeous.

But there had been something else to this woman, beyond her obvious sex appeal. She'd seemed...she'd seemed...oh, nightmare, here it came. She'd seemed *interesting*. And the Dreammakers were never supposed to become interested in humans. They were supposed to dance through their dreams, send them nightmares or pleasure-filled fantasies, but they were never, ever supposed to get involved beyond that. It just wasn't done. However, here Lilith was, thinking of this human woman, this "Isabelle," and wondering what she was doing at that moment.

Lilith had tried everything she could to distract herself that day. She'd stopped by the feast hall and eaten a large breakfast. She'd gone to multiple friends' houses and questioned all of them about their last dalliances in the dream world, doing her best to hide the fact that she wasn't speaking about hers for a single moment. She'd even tried to write a poem, but none of the words seemed right. Who on earth (or, rather, *not* on earth, in her case) would want to read a poem about lazy ducks? No one, no one at all, and so, finally, she gave up and decided to check on the woman who simply wouldn't leave her thoughts alone. She took a bowl from her cupboard and filled it with water from her sink, and placed it on her kitchen table. She sprinkled in a little lavender, a little ginger oil, and a few crumbled leaves from one of the eldwood trees. They were the most important part, as the rest just made the water smell good. Then she closed her eyes and spoke the words that would give her a view of the human world, three short words, After those three words came the most important one—a name she was already becoming quite fond of. "Isabelle."

She opened her eyes. There she was, Isabelle, yelling at a man and a woman about some kind of…had he been cheating on her? Was that it? And was he her boyfriend? Lilith had seen him in Isabelle's dreams before she stepped through the mirror and into the dream world. Isabelle and he (was his name Martin?) had been fighting about sex in the dream, and that was why Lilith had interrupted it. Well, that and the fact that Isabelle was so very much her type. Even if she wasn't Isabelle's, as Lilith had sensed a distinct lack of lesbian experience in the young woman.

Lilith continued to watch the fight as the two people left the apartment, the man seeming to be in a huge hurry. Isabelle went into the kitchen and mixed up a batch of something, a look of shock on her face the entire time she baked. Whatever it was she had made, it looked delicious, and it must have been, because Isa proceeded to eat a large amount of it. It was some kind of baked good, brown and dense.

Lilith thought it was cute that Isabelle was oblivious to the fact that she had a fair amount of it smeared across her face by the time she finished eating. Then Isabelle picked up a book and settled onto the couch, beginning to read. Ah, how lovely. Lilith loved to read, too, even sneaking books out of people's dreams sometimes (a definite no-no). The one Isa was reading was one Lilith was quite familiar with, one she almost knew by heart.

But then came a sudden sound—the meeting hall's bell. She quickly grabbed the bowl and dumped the water into the sink, watching the image of Isabelle as she slowly floated down the drain. What an intriguing woman.

But this was not the time to think of any woman. No, any time the meeting hall's bell rang, it called every one of her village's inhabitants to come to the hall, and they weren't supposed to dawdle on the way there. She grabbed her cloak from the door, draping it around her shoulders and pulling her hair out from underneath it. Even among the Dreammakers she had striking hair, the only one of her line of sexual Dreammakers to have hair that particular shade of red. The women whose dreams she entered would often remark upon it, something she had become accustomed to and which didn't really please her as intensely as it had a hundred years ago. No, these days it hardly pleased her at all. Well, this new development—this interest in the human woman—at least it would be an entertaining change.

She left her house and exited her yard, clicking the gate shut behind her. Strange that the bell was ringing so early. They usually didn't meet until a few hours before evening occurred in the city they brought dreams to. Hopefully nothing bad had happened. But upon entering the hall, as one of the last Dreammakers to walk into the large room, she could clearly see something big had occurred, and whatever it was, it was not good news. Their village's leader, Amaya, sat in her usual spot, a plain, high-backed chair in front of the many benches, and her expression was anything but happy. She was frowning a little as she sat there, scanning the room, and her usually straight, sleek hair looked as if it, like her, was in a state of distress. Lilith had never seen her look even slightly disheveled, so something was clearly not right. What could it be? Lilith settled into a seat and prepared to hear whatever Amaya had to say. The last of the women and men entered the hall and sat down, and Amaya began to speak.

"I have what I'm afraid is some very bad news. Someone who is not one of us has been entering people's dreams in our city, and he or she has not been doing good things."

"How do you know it isn't one of us?" one of the seated men asked.

"Yes," came a woman's voice. "No one else can control anyone's dreams except Dreammakers."

"That may have been true until now," Amaya said with the beginnings of a frown. "But someone has been swimming through the city's dreams and controlling the humans' waking lives through their dreams. I know no one among us would do such a thing, and that is why I am certain it is someone—or something—else. After all, I can enter the dreams each of you creates," she said, gesturing toward the crowd, "and I have searched through them, and I have not seen a single hint of anyone here taking over the dreams of the humans in such a way."

Lilith was practically shaking from the news. But was it from anger? Fear? Perhaps both.

Amaya continued to speak of what little she knew—that people were having horrific dreams, dreams they sometimes couldn't escape, dreams they became trapped in for the entire night, even sometimes not waking up from them at the sound of their alarm.

"I am planning to travel to Queen Rebecca's castle very soon. Now, it's time to return to your usual practices. It will be dreamtime in about eight hours, and there will be those who are napping during the day or afternoon. Bring them sweet dreams, my people, so they will not worry and so that they may relax and enjoy pleasure."

The Dreammakers all stood, heading toward the large doors behind all the benches. They would have to spread the word amongst the rest of them, the ones who were busy with humans who happened to be sleeping when the meeting was called. Lilith headed back toward her quarters, but halfway there, she felt a strange pull toward her mirror's room, and without hesitating for a second, she followed it there, shutting the door behind her. Without much more than a thought, the mirror began to display Isabelle, just lying down for a nap. Poor girl. It seemed rather important that, after her tough morning, she enjoy her sleep. She should enjoy it as much as humanly possible, Lilith decided, and so just as Isa drifted off on her couch, a thin blanket on top of her, Lilith stepped through the mirror and into Isabelle's dreams.

CHAPTER FOUR

Isa was back at the mansion. The cold air outside brought to her attention how little she was wearing, only a pair of white lace panties and a matching cupless lace bra, showing off her everything and then some. This time, she didn't hesitate—or knock—before she entered.

Once inside the large room past the hallway, where the orgy had been, she saw it now held only a single bed, with a gorgeous man and an equally gorgeous woman draped across it. The man was subtly muscled and fully nude, not even covered by the bed's soft-looking sheets. His head was shaved, and black ink decorated most of his body. But most noticeable were his startling gold eyes, staring holes through Isa's scraps of clothing.

The woman was his opposite, with lustrous, blond curls dripping down her elegant shoulders and halfway down her arms. And her eyes were gold as well. Both sets of eyes looked surprisingly familiar, actually. Had she seen eyes like that before? Possibly. But then, each of them reached out a beckoning hand, matching wicked smiles on their faces, smiles that drew her thoughts to other, more prurient things.

When she reached the bed, the woman said only one word, "Undress." Isa hesitated for mere seconds, then stripped off what little clothing she wore, the slight coolness of the room drawing her attention to the parts of her body that were warmer than the rest and the parts that were getting wet.

The man and woman leaned forward, and each took one of Isa's hands, pulling her onto the bed. The man's cock looked more than ready to please her any way she wished, or possibly in any way *he* wished, and she didn't care, really, which it was. She wasn't sure how she felt about the woman being there, though. Strangely, she almost seemed to draw Isa's attention a little more than the man did. Isa now started wondering about that. *I'm straight...aren't I?*

"Isa," he said, "I am Lane, and this is Leonora, and we would like to bring you pleasure, pleasure like you've never felt before."

"Tell us," Leonora said, trailing fingers down Isa's side, bringing her hand dangerously close to Isa's nipple and then even closer to the place where her thighs met. "Tell us. Have you ever been with two people at the same time before?"

"No, of course not."

"Of course not?" Lane chuckled.

Why is this so surprising to him? Maybe it was uncommon in this mansion to have never been in a threesome.

"Yes, never," Isa said, her cheeks heating up as she spoke.

"Well, then, you are in for a *treat*." Lenora brought her lips to Isa's and kissed her. Only moments later, Isa felt a hand brushing against her bush—Lane's. And then, as Leonora kissed her, Lane's fingers dipped lower, pushing past her bush and inside her pussy's lips, touching her everywhere between her legs except for her clit. Which, of course, was torture.

Isa pulled back from Leonora's lips for a moment, turning to Lane. "Please..." was all she got out of her mouth before he swept down to her pussy and placed his lips exactly where she'd been wishing to be touched. His tongue sent an electric jolt across her skin, and her back bowed a little, making her almost rise off the bed from the hard pressure of his tongue.

But then, Leonora shoved Isa onto her back, grasping each of her wrists in a small, strong hand, and stared down at her, lips wet and expression hungry.

"You know we're the ones in control," she said. "You know that, don't you?"

"Yes, yes." Isa's lips quivered as she felt the pressure of both Lane's tongue and Leonora's hands, as well as the pressure of Leonora's gaze. She stared into Isa's eyes, seeming to assess her, and Isa could tell then that any secret she wished to keep from Leonora would be a secret for mere seconds. "Is he…are you… is either of you going to fuck me?"

Lane raised his head from Isa's pussy, grinning up at her. "Oh, so she wants to be fucked, does she?"

"Yes, it seems she does."

"Easily taken care of." And with that, Lane climbed on top of her and Leonora writhed her way under, a shiny, black strap-on appearing on Leonora's crotch only moments before she got underneath Isa. Both dicks were dangerously close to where Isa desperately wanted them to be.

"How are you both…I mean, is one of you going to fuck my ass?" She was a little nervous at the thought, as she'd never had her ass penetrated before, not even by a finger.

"Hmm," Leonora said, reaching around Isa and squeezing her tight. "Well, why don't we just start with your pussy and work our way back from there?"

And before Isa could ask her—or actually, both of them— what she was wondering (how would they both fit?) each slid their dick inside her cunt, and fuck, but she'd never felt even close to that full before. Nor had she ever felt anything that delicious. She felt stretched taut around each of the dicks—one flesh, one not. And then they began to fuck her, and then, only moments later, she came, the fastest she'd ever come before. And goddamn, was it *ever* a good orgasm.

But as they thrust in and out of her, as she stared up into Lane's eyes, Isa remembered where she'd seen them before, where she'd seen golden eyes like his. They belonged to a gorgeous woman, one with garnet hair, one who had called her darling, upstairs in this very house.

"She's thinking of Lilith," Leonora said, and Lane grinned.

"Is it her that you want?" Lane asked.

"I…I don't know. Maybe. Yes." And then, Isa gasped as Leonora and Lane snapped out of existence, and then there she was, Lilith, walking toward the bed, draped in velvet and smiling.

Isa smiled back at her. "You're so beautiful."

But instead of thanking her, Lilith swore. "Fuck. Your phone's ringing. Damn it…there were things I wanted to say, and I wanted to talk to you, about stuff other than, well, sex. Can I see you again tonight? Will you welcome me into your dreams?"

"Certainly." It was the only correct answer. Lilith bent down, her hair trailing across Isa's breasts, and she ever-so-delicately cupped Isa's face and kissed her.

"To remember me by," Lilith said, and then, moments before their lips met, she whispered, "Enjoy your book. It's one of my favorites."

❖

And yet again, an annoying noise pulled Isa out of a wonderful sex dream and back into reality. At least she'd managed to have an amazing orgasm in this one. And amazingly hot sex. Sadly, she probably wouldn't have much of that in her real life for quite a while. Not with singleness looming over her like a dark storm, just getting ready to pelt her with ice-cold rain. Why did this strange, beautiful woman keep entering her dreams, though? That made two within mere hours. And why mention a book? Wasn't Lilith just supposed to look hot and seduce her a second time?

But her phone was ringing right now. She pushed herself into a mildly upright position and picked the phone off the table—the bamboo table she and Martin had found at a flea market a few months ago. Well, now that memory was completely tarnished.

"Yes?" she said, after pushing the "answer" button. "I mean, hello?"

"It's Toni, your favorite co-worker. How're you doin'?" Toni wrote for the same Web site as Isa, writing most of the articles about sexuality for the blog. She certainly was well-versed when it came to everything sexual, but that was just part of her charm.

"I've been...better, I suppose," Isa replied. *Time to drop the bomb.* "I just dumped Martin."

"Thank God." Toni cleared her throat. "Oops. I mean, I'm sorry. But I also meant 'thank God.' I just shouldn't have said it out loud."

Isa chuckled dryly. "Well, I spent most of the morning writing, but half the time I was wondering if I should leave him, you know, and then I saw Patricia walking toward our apartment, and then...then I went home, to see what was up. And apparently, for who knows how long, Martin and she have been..." She paused, not really sure how to phrase such an evil thing.

"I think I can put two and two together and come up with 'fucking.' Although maybe the correct answer is 'four.' I never was very good at math."

Isa smiled for real for the first time since she'd found out about Martin and Patricia. "Ding ding ding, and the prize goes to the lady with the crude choice of words. Yep, they've been doing just that, so I kicked him out and told him to pick up his stuff later. Told him that we were over, too. And then Patricia had the nerve to apologize."

"That sounds like her. Full of nerve and full of shit. Never liked the girl, don't know what you saw in her. Don't know what you saw in Martin, either. I *have* been telling you that for, I don't know, two years or so."

And she had, practically since Martin and Isa had met. Isa realized now that she should have listened. "Yes, you have, and yes…you were right, but I'm only saying that grudgingly."

"Well, I can't say I'm delighted that it ended over what it did, but I am definitely delighted that it ended. This is for good, right?"

"Oh, of course. Like I said, I was already halfway to dumping him."

"Well, this calls for a celebration, and what better way to celebrate than a date at our favorite watering hole? Maybe you can pick up a rebound while we're there."

"I think it's a little soon for that. Yes to the rest, though."

"Great! Don't be surprised if you run into a cute guy while we're out. Like, say, one of my friends. His name is Evan."

"Oh. Great."

"No, trust me, Isabelle, he's a total hunk. You'll thank me later."

"I will?"

"Definitely. Okay, well, I gotta get back to work. Duty calls. See you there at seven, okay?"

"Sure. Bye!"

Now Isa only had about, what, four whole hours to kill until then? Wonderful. Maybe a walk, something active to distract her. Yeah, that would probably do the trick. She put on some warmer clothes—a long-sleeved T-shirt Martin had never liked and some jeans and tennis shoes—then right before she left, she threw together a "fuck you and I'm glad we broke up" playlist for her MP3 player.

Once outside, she had to admit she didn't really know where she wanted to go. So she took off at a brisk pace in the opposite direction of the one she'd taken earlier that day. Her brisk pace changed to a slight jog, and soon her feet were pounding the pavement in time to the beat of the song she was listening to. Isa ran for quite a while, barely taking in the spring flowers and the people she passed, but by the time five songs had played she had to stop to catch her breath. And as luck would have it, she stopped just a few blocks short of her favorite museum in the city, a small part of why she'd chosen this area to live in. The exhibits changed more frequently here than they did in most of the other museums, and they always had an amazing variety of art, even outside of the visiting stuff on display. And as more luck would have it, today was the first Wednesday of the month, a free day at the MMFA. She pushed open one of the doors to the building and went inside.

This month's exhibit consisted of statues and paintings by an artist she'd never heard of—just Iriana, no last name. They were absolutely beautiful, all seeming to be of the same red-haired, curvaceous woman, but not a single one showed the woman's face. Each piece had, well, an *energy* to it, Isa realized, something otherworldly, maybe something ethereal. It was a delight to look at all of Iriana's art, and she spent a good hour—or more—meandering through the four rooms displaying it.

In the last room of the exhibit, though, she spotted a painting that stood out far more than the rest. In muted colors, all except for the woman's amazing hair—rich and beautiful red hair, yet another reminder of Isa's dreams. The woman's figure was similar to that of her dream woman as well, but her face was turned away, only the slightest hint of it visible. No, it would have been too strange if her face were in the painting, because then she possibly would have had a face like the woman Isa had been dreaming about, too. Isa laughed a little at the possibility that someone would paint a woman who was in her dreams.

Then she saw the security guard looking at her with an odd expression. She cleared her throat and left the room, a little embarrassed. Yes, maybe she was going a bit crazy, but she didn't really care. The dreams she'd had were certainly worth a little craziness. Especially if she dreamed about the woman again, Isa thought, then immediately tried to banish said thought. Why would she want to dream about Lilith again? It was just a dream, just something her brain came up with to help her sleep, or possibly process something.

She decided she might as well go through the rest of the museum, even though she'd seen everything else countless times. She lingered over her favorite paintings and photographs, most of them portraits, but she also studied a painting full of angry colors and amazing hills and valleys caused by the incredible thickness of the paint. Her last stop was the museum's café for a quick bite, since she didn't want to go to the bar on an empty stomach.

Now it was almost time to meet Toni, and she had to change into something a little more presentable, so she caught a bus home and chose a black wrap-around dress and ballet flats. No reason to look too snazzy, as she wasn't exactly going man-hunting tonight, despite what Toni thought she should do. No, she needed a break from men. She spritzed on a little of her favorite perfume, one that Martin had never liked, so she'd never worn it…how silly that seemed now. Well, now things were different. She left her apartment and hailed a cab, wondering exactly how "different" things would become now that she was single again.

CHAPTER FIVE

Once inside the bar, she didn't have much trouble spotting Toni. Isa had always thought of Toni's general style as "peacock couture." Tonight, she wore a short red-and-purple dress that left no question as to whether she had tits—or ass. And so of course plenty of men always flocked around her. It took her a few moments to notice Isa, but when she did, Toni sashayed over to her, a martini glass in her hand that held liquid matching the red of her dress. "Hey there, sexy!" She enveloped Isa in a one-arm hug, then pulled back. "You look great, Isabelle."

Toni was pretty much the only person who called Isa by her full first name. To everyone else, she was Isa, which she preferred. But of course, Toni was Toni, so she let her get away with it.

"Here." Toni draped an arm around Isa's shoulders. "Come to my booth and meet Evan."

They walked over to their usual booth, where a muscled, smiling man sat, his curly mop of dark-brown hair probably cut to show off his cheekbones. Okay, he was hot, Isa thought, although it looked like he knew it, too.

"Hi, I'm Isa," she said as she sat down.

It turned out that his good looks were about all he had going for him. Isa learned this only shortly after sliding into the booth next to him. She sipped her whiskey sour as he went on and on about the "big" deal he'd closed today. And then it was on to his workout regime. Isa almost felt like she might nod off while he talked. In the middle of his explanation about why he chose tanning booths over tanning spray, she told him she needed to use the restroom. Maybe splashing some cold water on her face would help stop the endless waves of boredom from lulling her to sleep.

She locked the door behind her, then turned on a faucet and let it run for a few moments. The huge mirror behind the sink covered the whole wall, and she took a second to look herself over in it. Strangely, her hair looked a little redder than usual—probably a trick of the light. Then she ducked down and splashed the icy water on her face, not caring in the least about messing up her makeup. By now, she didn't care at all whether Mr. Stockbroker Gym Nut thought she was hot. Then she looked up from the sink and screamed.

It wasn't herself she was looking at in the mirror, but a ghostly, floating face. Was this bathroom haunted? Then the face came more into focus, now much more solid looking, and Isa realized she was looking at the woman she'd been dreaming about. Was she asleep? It wouldn't be surprising, considering how dull her one-sided conversation with Evan had been. Well, this would most likely be another sex dream, which was certainly fine with her, although hopefully Evan wouldn't notice if she came. That would certainly send the wrong message.

"Hi," she said to the mirror. Or, rather, to the woman in it. "Lilith, right?"

"Yes, right," she said, smiling. Lilith wasn't wearing much, just a slightly translucent gown, hints of her nipples and her lower red hair peeking through the gauzy blue cloth.

"You look lovely. Am I dreaming right now?"

"Yes, you are. That Evan fellow seemed to be boring you to death, so I thought I'd see if I could push you over the edge between wakefulness and sleep. I hadn't known until now that I had that ability. Only our queen is supposed to be able to do that, but I seem to have some sort of strange connection to you. It's curious, admittedly. I don't usually get very interested in the women I bring dreams to, but *you* seem to have caught my interest…for some odd reason."

Well, this dream was certainly unusual, too. Apparently Isa was supposed to think Lilith was some kind of dream-creating goddess or something in this one. "I guess I should say 'thank you' for knocking me out. God, what an annoying guy."

"My, yes. He certainly is. I hope I don't annoy you in the same way. I don't think you seem to have a…*thing*…for women."

"No, not really. But you seem to be an exception. Are we… are we going to have sex now? I wouldn't mind, not at all." She got ready for Lilith to come through the mirror and for Lilith to begin to undress her. What would Lilith do to her this time?

"I was hoping…" A very shy-looking expression crossed Lilith's face as she paused. "I was hoping I could get to know you a little, actually."

Well, now, Isa thought, *that* was surprising. "You were hoping to get to know me? Okay, sure. What do you want to know?"

"What are your…interests? What do you like to do?" Now a chair appeared behind Lilith, somewhat throne-like, with a high back and a black finish. She sat down on it, crossing her legs, every movement more sensual than the last.

"What do I like to do? Well, I love to read, as you seem to already know from what you said in my last dream. Especially poetry and historical fiction. My favorite poet is—"

"Edna St. Vincent Millay? Mine as well. She does such lovely things with the English language."

"Yeah, she does." She would have asked Lilith how she knew, but of *course* Isa's subconscious was aware of her sizeable Millay collection.

"What's your favorite poem of hers?" Lilith leaned forward expectantly.

"'I Think I Should Have Loved You Presently.'"

Lilith grinned at this answer. "Mine as well! Oh, what a lovely poem. I'm so happy to hear that. What else can you tell me about yourself?"

Isa was starting to like this strange dream-woman. Maybe she'd still get some joy out of her dreams, at least, since her waking life wasn't all sunshine and bunnies at the moment. It would be better than no fun at all, even if it still was all imaginary and entirely outside of real life. The sex parts of her dreams of Lilith were great, but she enjoyed talking to this gorgeous woman as well. Although it didn't exactly hurt that she could see through Lilith's dress.

"What else...hmm. Well, I'm not very athletic, but I love to swim. It's one of my favorite ways to exercise."

"Yes, I love swimming also. A dip in our rivers is always delightful."

"You have rivers where you live? What else is there?" Now Isa was curious. Even if this was just a dream, it was still a very interesting one. God, the things her subconscious came up with. At least it was being generous on this occasion, not giving her one of those awful recurring nightmares she'd had for years. The ones with the creature who chased her down dark streets, through dark fields, the dreams that came with a heavy dose of insomnia after jolting her awake.

"Recurring nightmares?" Lilith asked. Oh, so she could read Isa's mind. *But of course she can, dummy! All of this is coming from your mind!* "I'll have to see if I can talk to the nightmare Dreammakers, see if we can get rid of them. What was I saying, though...yes, rivers. What else is there? Oh, we have gardens, full of flowers, always in bloom. Flowers you have on earth and many you don't.

"My favorites are the votive plumes. They smell like your jasmine, but they're a rich blue and glow brightly at night. Sometimes we pick one and use it to explore the garden after the sun has gone down. They put off light for a good few days. Oh, I would so love to show you them someday, but I'm afraid we're confined to just talking in your dreams. But I can bring one into this dream, of course!" She waved her hand, then a short stem appeared in it, topped by glowing blue shoots of star-shaped flowers.

"It's beautiful, Lilith. Just beautiful. How nice of my imagination to come up with such pretty things."

"Your...imagination. I would suppose you wouldn't understand that it's not your imagination that is creating this dream. It makes me sad, but maybe there's some way for me to prove it to you. Oh! Maybe I can use my skill at pulling things out of dreams and put something...yes! Check your bedside table when you get home. Something will be waiting for you there. A gift."

"Well, it's been delightful talking to you, Lilith, but I should probably wake up now."

"Oh, but don't you want a little pleasure before you awaken?" Her voice had changed its tone, a subtle shift, but one that Isa's body noticed in an instant. "Here," Lilith said, and she reached through the mirror and placed something in Isa's hand. It glowed like the flowers, but it most certainly wasn't a flower. No, it was a pale-blue dildo. And moments later, a chair like Lilith's appeared to Isa's right. Then, just as suddenly, Isa was completely naked. She watched, with just a touch of awe, as Lilith pushed up her skirt and began to rub her clit. Her lower lips were flushed a dark pink, showing clearly how aroused she already was. "Sit," Lilith said, moaning a little after the word. "Sit and touch yourself for me."

It was pretty much impossible for Isa to turn down an invitation like that, at least coming from Lilith, so she sat in the chair and spread her legs wide, placing each one over an armrest, giving Lilith as clear a view as possible. Isa was getting very aroused too, just by watching the dream woman touch herself. Did she suddenly have a thing for women? Was that what these dreams meant? Well, she'd have plenty of time to worry about that later. Right now, all she wanted was to watch Lilith. Well, that and to come.

Isa was already slick and wet, so the dildo slid in easily, filling her with its rigid, thick length in mere seconds. She began to fuck herself with it, slowly at first, then quickening her pace. She'd never been able to come from penetration alone, but something about this time felt different. It felt better, better than penetration ever had, her whole cunt coursing with sensation, and she couldn't hold back for very long. Soon she was panting, moaning, squeezing her eyes and furrowing her brow, but she still tried as best she could to watch Lilith touch herself, and then, soon—*too* soon—Isa was arching her back, as was Lilith, and they both came, loudly, their cries echoing in the small bathroom.

As Isa slowly slid the dildo out of her over-sensitized cunt, she smiled at Lilith. "Thanks, dream woman. That was… amazing. Will I see you again?"

"Soon, I hope. I think I have an assignment tonight, but maybe sometime tomorrow. Could you work in a nap, perhaps?"

"For you, anything." Isa grinned widely, and soon Lilith was grinning, too.

"Time to wake up now, darling."

❖

Evan was shaking Isa's shoulder. She slowly lifted her head up from the table, wiping off a touch of drool that she was certain was *very* attractive to Evan. Not that she really cared whether this boring, boring man thought she was hot. No, not in the least.

"You, uh, fell asleep, Elise." He looked somewhat surprised, like he couldn't possibly imagine someone falling asleep in his awesome company.

"Isa, it's Isa." She guessed she had a very stupid grin on her face, but not from Evan. Oh, no. And now something was clearly necessary—she had to get home and get off. Because she certainly wasn't going to use Evan when her trusty vibrator was more interesting than he was. More interesting and *far* more likely to get her off.

She located Toni, yet again surrounded by mostly men (and a few annoyed-looking women), and got ready to beg off. "I'm really tired, Toni. I fell asleep at the table, actually. I need to get home."

"It's only eleven, Isabelle! The night is young! Are you sure?"

"Yep, I'm exhausted." Exhausted and horny as fuck, but Toni didn't need to know that part. After all, if Isa *had* told her that, Toni might try to get her to take Evan home. *And sorry, but...ick.*

"Well, I'm planning to sleep when I'm dead, so I'll be out a while longer. Lunch in a few days, though, perhaps?" she said, wiggling her eyebrows. "Guess Evan didn't cut your cake like I thought he would."

Chuckling, Isa told Toni that she'd be happy to join her for lunch, as long as Evan wasn't invited. But at the moment, her bed was calling her—and so was her vibrator.

CHAPTER SIX

L ilith did indeed have an assignment that night. Apparently the man Amaya had left in charge, Francisco,
wanted her to enter a man's dream. Which was horrible of him,
but still excusable, since she wasn't out to him. No, Francisco
couldn't have known how unappealing that would be for her.
Well, if she made this man a woman in the dream, maybe it would
become palatable. She didn't mind taking on the role of a man
in a woman's dream, but bring the opposite into play—make her
into a dream woman for someone with a real-life dick—and that
was…well, she didn't know enough words that could even begin
to describe her complete and utter distaste.

In the dream, she made the man (who, to make matters
worse, was not even close to attractive in his waking life) into
a gorgeous woman, with curves that could kill and cheekbones
you could cut yourself on. She had short-cropped, spiky hair,
and Lilith made sure it was soft and pliable. Pliable, just like she
made him—now *her*.

They were lying on a blanket under the stars, sharing a
bottle of brandy, each of them holding a large-bowled, stemmed
drinking glass. And then, as a last-minute idea crossed Lilith's
mind, the woman began to change shape, her face changing as
well, and then she looked quite different, with curly black hair
and a face that was growing quite familiar to Lilith by now.

"They're beautiful, aren't they?" the woman said a few seconds later. "So many stars."

"You're just as beautiful as they are, darling." Lilith placed her glass on a plot of flat ground to her right, then took the woman's glass from her, downing the last swallow and then put it next to its twin. "Would you like to take off your clothes?"

"It's a little cold, but…yes, I would." The woman stood and stripped off her dress and underwear, revealing hard nipples and a dark bush.

Lilith pulled her back down and climbed on top of her, shoving her hand against the woman's crotch. "What do you like?" Lilith asked her.

"Well, I don't really know." The woman bit her lower lip in a quite appealing way, and Lilith decided she just had to kiss her. She pressed her lips against the woman's, tasting hints of the brandy—rich, full, and strong.

"You taste delicious," Lilith told her. "Now I want to taste the rest of you." She kissed her way down the woman's body, pausing to nip her flesh in a few places—her left hip, her upper thighs—and then she took each thigh and slowly spread the woman's legs, revealing her wet cunt to the cool night air. Lilith blew softly between the woman's lower lips, causing a sigh, then a slight shudder. Then she placed her face closer and tasted the woman's cunt for the first time, the woman gasping, then moaning and clenching her thighs.

"I've never done this before, you know," the woman said. Lilith already knew this, but those words never failed to turn her on, and she began to get wet as well. Since she had all the control in the world (or at least, in *this* world), Lilith was suddenly naked, and as she licked away, she reached down and began to touch her own cunt, moaning into the woman's wetness, her sounds vibrating against the woman's clit.

Lilith used her other hand to stroke the woman's labia, the woman's flesh soft against her fingers. Then she slowly slid her hand down, rubbing her finger against the woman's delicate, delicious spot between her asshole and her cunt. Lilith brought her finger farther back, pressing down a little on the woman's tight, tight hole. She slowly began to slip her finger inside, until it was in all the way, bringing a cry of "Oh, God!" from the woman, and bringing a smile to Lilith's face. She began to fuck the woman's ass with her finger, slipping it in and out with ease. No need for lubrication in a dream, as Lilith could make almost everything—every bit of scenery, every body part—do anything she wanted, which was almost always a delight.

Lilith had started out slow, but now she ramped it up, giving it all she had, because she was close, so close, and she knew the woman was, too. Speeding up her tongue, she also sped up the fingers on her own clit, sped up the finger sliding in and out of the woman's ass, and soon enough they were both coming, their sounds flowing through the cool night air.

❖

Lilith walked out of the mirror. She felt a little off, for some reason. Off, but maybe she actually felt even further discomfort, something more than just "off." Yes, she felt upset. Had she... cheated? No, not really. She and Isa had no possibility for such an agreement. But still she had stronger feelings for this woman, this Isa, stronger feelings that grew every time she went into the woman's dreams. Turning the man into Isa had helped, but that was merely a bandage, a poorly applied one, merely a slight covering of a lust that bled out of her very bones. But was it just lust? No, it certainly wasn't. It was something more, and it would certainly only continue to get worse.

She went back to her quarters and prepared for bed—washing her face, brushing her hair, and changing out of her dress and into a silk pajama set. She opened the window in her bedroom. The room felt stuffy, but maybe that was just her. She had a tightening in her chest, but not an entirely unpleasant one. Almost like something was pulling her, pulling her toward something. Or someone.

CHAPTER SEVEN

After getting home, Isa hurried into her bedroom, stripping off her clothes and opening her bedside drawer. She wouldn't be needing the condoms at all for God knew how long, but luckily, she still had the only thing that could take care of things in the interim. Removing her vibrator from the drawer, she clicked it on and placed it on her clit. Now—what to fantasize about?

She started with one of her standards: herself lying nude on a bed in a dimly lit room. A man stood at the edge of the bed, naked, staring down at her, his eyes drinking her in. She watched as he climbed onto the bed and...

No, strangely, that one wasn't working for her. *Huh.*

Now she was in a room full of men, each of them leering at her, all of them with their dicks ou...

No, not that one either. Had she switched teams? Because the next fantasy that popped into her head starred two women. And that one was *definitely* doing it for her.

They were lying next to her, one on each side, each of them with a dildo in her hand.

"Suck it," said the woman on the right, Amy (because apparently, she deserved a name). Amy placed the flesh-colored dildo on Isa's lips, slowly sliding it into her mouth, and then Amy began to fuck Isa's face. Drool pooled around the rubber dick, dripping down her cheeks. Oh, this was definitely doing it for her. Her clit felt like it was on fire.

The other woman, Jen (*why another name?*) slid down Isa's body while Amy fucked her face, and Jen began to lick her pussy. Isa moaned around the dildo in her mouth, and Amy grinned, staring down at her. "What a dirty, dirty little whore you are, you fucking *slut*."

Jen continued to lick Isa's pussy, and then she removed her lips and slid the dildo she held inside of Isa, stretching her wide. It wasn't small, and Isa could barely take it all. In fact, it hurt a little…but in a rather good way.

The two women began to fuck her in tandem, one fucking her face, the other fucking her pussy, and Jen's tongue returned to Isa's clit.

Then Amy yanked the dildo out of Isa's mouth and climbed up the bed, straddling her face, and shoved her cunt against Isa's lips. So what could Isa do, but begin to lick her cunt, her tongue sliding up and down its slippery surface, tasting every bit of her. And did she ever taste delicious…which reminded Isa of the dream woman's pussy, so sweet, so lovely, and as Isa thought of the taste, her orgasm pulled her out of the fantasy, and she moaned and shook all the way through it.

Sated for now, Isa started getting ready for bed, trying to ignore the fact that she'd just gotten off to a fantasy involving women for the very first time. After all, she could always work on figuring it out tomorrow, but now she needed to think about going to sleep.

As she washed her face in the bathroom, she paused her scrubbing for a moment, staring at her reflection in the mirror. Strangely, she felt almost like it would have been nice to see her dream woman in this mirror. Maybe Isa would dream about her tonight, even though her subconscious probably had other plans. Hopefully, she'd see Lilith in her sleep and wouldn't have another of her nightmares instead, the ones that came every few weeks, the ones that had been happening since she was a little kid. She couldn't even remember a time when they hadn't come to her, and they certainly weren't enjoyable. No, Isa prayed she wouldn't have one tonight.

But, of course, she did.

❖

Isa was running, running as fast as she could. The creature was the reason she was running—the terrifying creature who had been stalking her for years. Would he catch up to her this time, though? She really, really hoped not.

He was behind her, now, closing in on her—*fast*. He was already far too close, his horrible voice only a few yards behind her. "I'm not going to hurt you!" he called, his voice reaching out to her, almost like he could trap her with the sound of it alone. The same words, every time, the words that always sent shivers rippling across her skin.

"I just want to be free! Let me out, you bitch!" Now he was getting closer, his footfalls slowing, each tap of his shoes sounding more and more certain, each step seeming to state the fact that he would catch her this time, that this time he would finally win.

Isa couldn't help it. She screamed, then began to cry out for help. But all the houses on the street were dark. And then, suddenly, one lit up. Fire—it was burning, the flames bright against the dark night sky. She wanted to help the people inside, but if she stopped running, he would catch up and kill her, even though he said he wouldn't. So she sent out a thought to the building. It was the best she could do.

Please, anyone who's inside, run! Run before you catch on fire! Run!

❖

Then she woke up, her body covered in sweat, gasping for breath.

And only moments later, Isa heard the distinct sound of fire engines.

No, no way were the two connected. *No* way at all. It was just a bad dream, and her subconscious had probably just added the fire.

She reached for her bedside lamp and turned it on, and then the night got even weirder. A book lay there. A book she most certainly hadn't put there, as she didn't even own it. Edna St. Vincent Millay's first collection of poetry. It was obviously a very old copy but in absolutely pristine condition.

She was still trying to catch her breath, but she slowly reached out and touched it. Yes, it was real, the smooth leather binding soft and supple underneath her fingers. How had it gotten there? Was she still dreaming? And if she wasn't, what on *earth* was going on?

Chapter Eight

A number of blocks away from Isa's apartment, a man named Harold was dreaming.

❖

Harold was in his vacation cottage, and it was a dark, cold winter night, and he felt incredibly alone. He wanted to wish for some sort of company, but the only person within miles was not company anyone in their right mind would wish for. The man... the creature...Harold was praying that he hadn't followed him here. The creature was obviously not good news. No, he was stories of floods and hurricanes, murders and torture. He was not someone you'd want to follow you anywhere.

Luckily for Harold, there was a fireplace in his cabin, with a pile of wood and matches, so he bent down and struck a match, lighting the newspaper on top of the logs. *Ah, much better.* He doubted the smoke would lead the man to him, but still, he shouldn't let the fire burn for very long.

Soon enough, the cabin was heating up nicely. A few moments of enjoying the warmth, and then Harold realized it was getting a little *too* warm. It was getting uncomfortable, actually, and now, smoke was beginning to fill the room.

Then, somewhere outside, he heard a woman's voice, and
the sound of running feet. "Please, anyone who's inside, run!
Run before you catch on fire! Run!"

Now the fire had spread from the fireplace, no longer
contained, and a shove of the cabin's door showed he had no way
out. It had to be the creature. He must have noticed the smoke,
must have noticed the flames. Somehow, the creature had found
him, and now Harold was going to die in this cabin.

But was it too late? No, as luck would have it, he saw a phone
across the room. He picked it up and dialed 911. "Please, come
quick, there's a fire. It's spreading and I don't know what to do.
Please, hurry!" Then he felt himself getting weaker, weaker still,
and he collapsed, hoping and praying that the monster wouldn't
get in before he could be saved.

Orion was driving his normal route when he heard his
girlfriend Marianne's voice on his radio. "Orion, just thought you
should know, direct from your sweetie, that we have a 10-59 on
18th and Ashby. A private home is burning, and we have a trauma
team and a fire-control team on their way. Think you could stop
by there?"

Orion picked up his radio. "Gotcha, Marianne. I'm on my
way. Hey, can we meet up after work? Get an early breakfast at
our diner?"

"Sure thing, sugar."

Orion turned left and started toward Ashby. Hopefully
whoever the poor suckers were would only lose their home to
the fire, and not their lives. If they were lucky, the fire truck and
ambulance would arrive on time. If they weren't…

As Orion headed toward his destination, he decided to do
what he always did, so he said a silent prayer that help would
arrive in time.

❖

Harold came back to consciousness as two sets of arms grabbed his torso and legs. Oh, he felt so weak. What on earth had happened? And why was he surrounded by smoke? What the *hell* was going on?

Once outside, he was hurried out to an ambulance, an oxygen mask was placed on his face, and then they drove off in the early morning light, the siren telling everyone on the street that something had gone very, very wrong.

CHAPTER NINE

I n the morning, Isa woke up with a bit of a headache. She had managed to get back to sleep after a while, but said sleep had been fitful, and not exactly deep. She didn't usually get any more rest after one of her recurring nightmares, but something had been slightly different last night, something that made her feel…feel…safer, perhaps? *Strange.*

But that was just the beginning of "strange," because the Millay book was still on her bedside table, on top of a few old *National Geographic*s. And it looked decidedly solid and real in the early morning light. A few moments later, the beeping of her alarm clock made her jump, and then she practically leapt out of bed. She wanted to be in a room where that book wasn't, that book that should *not* have been there, the book that had no reason to be on her bedside table, in this reality. They had all just been dreams, right? The ones with the gorgeous woman in them? Just sex dreams—very hot ones—but not real, oh no, not like that book.

Was she hallucinating? Or had Martin put that book there, perhaps as a gift? No, because it hadn't been there when she'd left the apartment yesterday afternoon, and she had no reason to think he'd been back since then. Beyond that, it was far too much of a coincidence that he'd buy her that particular book, when she'd just dreamed about the woman and they'd had that conversation about Millay last night at the bar. And it most certainly hadn't been there when she got home. No, all of this was far too weird. It just didn't make any sort of sense.

"They're just dreams," Isa muttered. "Just dreams." Great, now she was officially going crazy. Talking to herself and hallucinating things, things from out of her dreams, things that landed in Isa's reality and came out of…Lilith's. Lilith, who was suddenly seeming slightly more real. And "slightly" turned to "extremely," as Isa walked over to her bedside table and gingerly reached out, feeling a very solid book underneath her hand. *Might as well pick it up, then.* She grasped the volume and did just that, then had the very strange urge to sniff it. Hmm, it smelled like…jasmine? Only slightly different from jasmine, though. Just slightly.

Isa put on her robe and belted it, putting down the book for a second while she adjusted the belt, then picked it back up and went into her kitchen. She pulled out a chair from the kitchen table and slowly, gently, eased the book open.

She noticed a pale-purple slip of paper, folded in half, inside the cover. When she opened it, the words inside shocked her even more than the book's appearance had. She drew her empty hand to her face, covering a mouth that had fallen open.

My darling,

I really enjoyed our talk last night. I hope you will think of me as you read the poems in this volume, and don't worry. The person whose dreams I took it from seems to never make time to read. I'm sure it's in much better hands now.

Looking forward to our next encounter,
Lilith

None of the thoughts in Isa's head managed to get even slightly close to completion, so she decided to prepare breakfast. Maybe a full stomach would help her deal with whatever the hell was going on. She got out the necessary ingredients for pancakes and whipped up a batch, then made some coffee for the headache that had only gotten worse with each unexplainable event—the book, and the note. Now, hours after that horrible nightmare, the book's appearance—and solidity—should have been almost equally upsetting. But something about it had a strange, calming effect on her.

After breakfast, she went into the living room and sat on the couch. Some work-related writing needed to happen today, but instead of getting out her laptop, she opened the book, carefully placed the note on the table next to the phone, and lost herself in Millay's words for a few hours.

The sound of a loud truck driving by shook her out of her haze. She'd been picturing Lilith almost the entire time she'd been reading, wondering if she, too, had sat somewhere and read this book with the same amount of joy. But then she shook her head at the thought. There was no Lilith, of course not. Yes, there had to be some other explanation. Had she told anyone at all about the dreams, though? No, she hadn't. And did she happen to have any psychic friends? No, she didn't. So maybe, just maybe, there really *was* a Lilith.

And then, bringing her almost fully out of thoughts of Lilith, Isa's computer beeped—a new e-mail. It was from Martin, who said he wanted to come by and talk to her, and maybe try to work this out.

It was easy enough to figure out what to write back to him— just a three-word sentence.

Go to hell.

And then, right before Isa clicked "send," she decided to add a suggestion that he start picking up his stuff in a couple of hours. She wrote that he could let himself in, and that she wouldn't be back until four. Hopefully he would understand that she wanted him gone before then.

Isa changed into some jeans and an untucked, button-up blouse. Her laptop went into its bag, and she got her keys, but at the last second a silly thought entered her head. She ducked back into the bathroom and spritzed on some perfume—jasmine-scented.

Outside, the weather was nice enough—slightly warm, with a sky covered in pale clouds. Where did she want to go, though? She walked a few blocks down to the nearest bus stop, and in an action that seemed surprisingly right, she got onto the first bus that came along. It was going to the most gay-friendly area of the city, which might have been why the decision had seemed so right.

Isa watched the trees and houses rush past as the bus moved along, trying to figure out the book's arrival in her apartment, and the note that had come with it. She hadn't thought of a single good answer by the time the bus stopped on Lincoln Avenue, where she decided to disembark.

As she walked down Lincoln for a few blocks, she took in the rainbow flags, the men holding hands, and the women, too. It was the first time she'd even thought to check out women as she strolled along one of the city's streets, and as she did, some of the women seemed to check her out as well.

At the end of the third block, she spotted a café named Milk and Cookies. Isa thought of how nice it might be for Vivian to have a place here, where she could be as out as her customers. The cheery scene she could see through the open windows and the scent of fresh brewed coffee drew her inside.

The place was certainly queer-friendly. In the dessert case, the cupcakes had rainbows on top, and among some T-shirts hanging from the wall behind the counter one said LEATHER DADDY 4 LIFE, and another one said MILK AND COOKIES—QUEERING IT UP SINCE 1982. Isa thought of buying that one for Vivian, but then she realized Vivian probably wouldn't really have too many occasions to wear it, considering how under wraps she kept her orientation.

Once Isa reached the front of the line, she ordered a mocha and a veggie sandwich from the barista, who had what Isa believed was called a fauxhawk, and each of her arms was covered in tattoos. She was not Isa's type, not really (did she even have a type yet?), but the barista still had a very attractive face—full lips, although they had a lip ring on each side, and beautiful, blue-green eyes.

After Isa ordered, she was given a wooden block with the number eleven on it. Only one empty table was left, so that was where she sat. The place was really full, and just as she sat down, a woman holding a mug full of coffee walked up to her.

"I'm sorry, but this seems to be the only seat left." The woman smiled at her (a rather charming smile, Isa thought), then asked, "Any chance you wouldn't mind sharing your table?"

"No, not at all, go ahead."

The woman sat down across from her, and Isa tried to check her out as subtly as she could. Her black hair was cut short, each side coming down at an angle, and she looked to be a little older, with laugh lines on each side of her dark-brown eyes that hinted at her age. Isa watched as she took a book out of her bag—David Sedaris's *Me Talk Pretty One Day*.

"That's a great book," Isa said, before her shyness stopped her from saying any more.

"Yeah, Sedaris is a hilarious guy. I'm Ming, nice to meet you…"

"Isabelle," Isa told her. "But everyone calls me Isa. And I hate to be impolite, but I need to get some writing done for work. So, if you don't mind?"

"Oh, not at all. I have David to keep me company." Ming grinned, her eyes crinkling up in a rather delightful way. She cracked open her book and began to read, and Isa got out her computer.

After she finished her eighth post for the day, almost three hours had passed, and she was surprised to see that Ming was still sitting across from her, still reading. She'd gotten up a few times, probably to refill her coffee, but other than that, she hadn't budged. Isa wondered why she might still be there, but she certainly knew what a good book could accomplish in terms of shooing away boredom (and responsibilities).

She closed her computer and put it back in its bag. Ming had taken out another book by now, apparently done with the Sedaris. This one was certainly not familiar to Isa, as it looked to be in Chinese. At least, that was what she guessed by the characters on the front.

Ming seemed to notice that Isa was getting ready to leave, looking up from her book, and she opened her mouth, about to say something, then seemed to decide against it.

"Well, I'm out now. Gotta head home. My ex should be done getting rid of his stuff by now."

"*His* stuff?" Ming asked, emphasizing the first word. She sounded surprised and, Isa thought, possibly a little disappointed.

"Yeah, but I'm kinda done with men for now." Did she really mean that?

"Oh, so you're...bi. That works, I suppose. You have any plans for dinner tonight?"

"No. No, none."

"Well, where do you live? Maybe I could meet you somewhere near there for dinner."

Was Ming asking her out? "I...live on Fir. West Fir. About fifteen blocks from the MMFA."

"They have a great Indian restaurant near there, Khanna—"

"Khanna Kuisine. That misspelled second word has always bugged me."

Ming laughed. "A grammar queen, huh? I think it's cute, actually."

"Cute, huh? I guess you could look at it that way." Isa stood up and slung her bags over her shoulder. "Okay, well, how about dinner at seven?"

"Sounds great, Isa. See you then."

Wow, Isa thought as she walked to the bus stop. She was going on her first, real, genuine lesbian date. But she didn't feel all that nervous. It felt *right* somehow, like it was meant to be. But what about Lilith—and her gift? If only she could enter into this world and...but no, Lilith was just a part of Isa's subconscious, trying to tell her something (that Isa was a lesbian?) She didn't really exist.

The book, though, the one which had appeared on her bedside table—that left Isa wondering about how close to existing Lilith really was. The thought tumbled around in her brain the entire bus ride home.

CHAPTER TEN

One day after the meeting she'd led in the meeting hall, the sexual Dreammakers' leader Amaya had left their village and entered the mirror to travel from her village to her destination, but now she was finally here, at the center of all the various villages of Dreammakers—the Palace of Dreams, where their current queen resided and ruled over them all. Amaya had always been quite fond of Queen Rebecca, and Rebecca had always been fond of her. So even though she had traveled here for a rather awful reason, it would still be a pleasure to visit with her friend.

After climbing the stairs of the massive marble building, Amaya knocked on the front door. She grinned when Cillian answered the door. He was the king, Rebecca's partner in everything, and also her first (and seemingly last) love. They had been together for almost a century, and although Cillian's hair was only dotted with gray, his face was starting to show his age, fine lines appearing across the once-young skin. Amaya wasn't all that young herself, and even though aging went slower in the world all Dreammakers resided in, they still aged, and they still could die. Amaya just hoped she would still have a fair number of years to continue spending time with Rebecca. She made a mental note to try to come here more often, but sadly, her duties as leader of her village made it nearly impossible to travel this far without a special reason.

Today's trip certainly had a special reason, but not one that Amaya was looking forward to talking about. She wished that she and Rebecca could just visit and enjoy each other's company, but that was not to be. Maybe the next visit could be more joyful, but today the business at hand was anything but.

"Cillian, it is *so* wonderful to see you again."

Cillian grinned, encircling her in a tight hug. "It's wonderful to see you too, Amaya. What brings you here today?"

"I'm afraid it isn't good news. Not good at all. Is Rebecca available to meet with me?"

"With you, certainly. Especially since it sounds important. Is there a problem in your city?" His look changed to one of concern.

Amaya grimaced a little at the question. "Yes, a big one, and I'm hoping that Rebecca can help."

"I hope so as well. She's in the kitchen right now, having a snack. Not the best meeting place, but will it do?"

"I'm a little hungry, actually," Amaya said with a slight smile.

"Then it's the perfect spot for your meeting. Here, follow me."

They began walking down the first of the long hallways that led to the back of the palace, and the kitchen. Normally, Amaya would have stopped to take in her favorite paintings and tapestries, as the walls were covered with art, but she didn't have time. This visit was too important. And admittedly, the offer of some likely-to-be-delicious food certainly didn't slow her feet.

Upon arriving at the kitchen's door, Cillian pushed it open, then kissed her on the cheek. "Will I see you again before you leave?"

"I'd love that, but I don't have time. I need to get back to our village…I need to solve this problem, and I need to solve it quickly."

"What problem?" Rebecca was sitting at a large table, and she had just turned her head toward the door, a piece of bread raised halfway to her mouth. "Oh, Amaya! Welcome!" She dropped her bread and rushed over to her friend, kissing her on each cheek and then pulling Amaya into a warm, gentle hug.

"Come, sit down. And eat, if you want, too. Are you hungry?" Rebecca gestured toward the table.

They walked over to where Rebecca had been sitting. "You've cut your hair!" Amaya said.

Rebecca's now-short hair was barely chin-length, her tight, perfect curls making a lovely, silver halo around her head. Her hair had been incredibly long before, but Amaya fell in love with the new length only moments after first laying eyes on it. It seemed to state what she had always known about her friend—that Rebecca was tough, a force to be reckoned with, although the lovely curls in her hair seemed to show her gentle side as well. Amaya almost shook her head at the thought. She was reading a *little* too much into what was just a new hairdo.

Rebecca touched a few strands of her hair, almost as if she still wasn't used to it being so short. "I just thought it would be fun. Besides, that's what the human women do when their hair goes gray. Or, at least, most of them."

"I like it, actually. But after so many years of seeing you with hair all the way down your back, it's still surprising. You haven't taken on any other 'human' habits since I last saw you, have you?"

"Well, there are these things the humans are always eating called 'cheeseburgers' that seem delightful. I've been wanting to get our cook to prepare one, but he says only uncivilized people eat them, that they would just make me fat, and so far he's completely against making them. But maybe you could offer a trade—a dream of your particular specialty, perhaps?"

"That could possibly be arranged." Amaya turned her lips up into a wry smile, but let her face fall only seconds later.

"What is it, Amaya? Is something wrong? I suppose you didn't just come to visit, then, or you would have sent word." Rebecca's brow furrowed as she sat back down on the stool near her food. "Here, sit. You can have some of the cheese and bread, if you're hungry. I'll have the cook prepare you something special for supper tonight, too. Now, tell me what has brought you here."

As Amaya sat down, Rebecca poured her some wine from a decanter, passing the glass across the table. Amaya took it with a hand that was shaking slightly. She took a long swallow, hoping it would calm her nerves.

Amaya began to tell Rebecca what had been going on. Her friend sat there, silently, as Amaya spoke, then put up her hand when Amaya assured her that none of her village's Dreammakers were the ones controlling the humans and their dreams. "Not that any of your village's people would do such a thing, but all of us Dreammakers are obviously the only ones who can control dreams. Perhaps…perhaps one of the Nightmaremakers for your humans' city did this, but…still, it doesn't seem possible that even *they* would stoop so low, despite how horrific their dreams can be. And very few of us have enough power to cause things to happen on earth in areas outside of dreams. Yes, we can plant ideas, but that's usually the only control the lower Dreammakers have over the human world. There has to be something else, something we've never seen before, because even in my extensive studies of our history, I've never read of such a thing."

"Nor have I, Rebecca. And my studies have been almost as vast and deep as your own. Between the two of us, surely we can bring up something from our memories that will explain this. I will not just stand idly by as these horrors are committed using *our* powers. I will not!" Amaya's attention was drawn to the fact that she was now clenching both of her fists tightly, and Rebecca put her own hands on top of each fist, massaging Amaya's hands with small, gentle movements.

"My dear, you must calm down. Nothing good has ever been accomplished with rage leading the charge. Nothing." She slowly let go of Amaya's hands, leaving them a little more relaxed than they had been moments before.

"I know, Rebecca, of course I know, but this is just... completely unacceptable."

"And I agree, Amaya. Something must be done. We must get to the bottom of this mystery."

Both of them were thinking the same thought, but neither dared to speak it aloud: was it already too late? They both did their best to push that worry out of their minds, but Amaya picked at her bread, and Rebecca twirled her wine goblet in her hands, back and forth, back and forth. Both were completely lost in thought for a few moments.

Then Rebecca bolted up. "Of course!"

"What is it? Did you come up with a solution?"

"Not a solution, exactly, though it may be worth something, at least. I had forgotten, as my daughter had mentioned it just in passing, but recently, she noticed—felt, actually—a sense of power from your humans' city, something strong, something old. Perhaps that is who is causing all of this...this..." Rebecca couldn't find an appropriate word for the awful acts that had been committed under the Dreammakers' watch.

"It hasn't gotten too bad, yet," Amaya said, wanting to reassure Rebecca as best she could. "Nothing's ever gone beyond repair, at least so far. We don't really know the extent of the damage that's been done, but it obviously hasn't reached fever pitch, not yet. We would certainly know if it had. Some things are impossible to miss, even up here, even in our world, far away from the humans. I know we aren't supposed to care about them as much as we care about fellow Dreammakers, but I'm afraid I fail miserably in that respect."

"As do I, as my husband and daughter are well aware." She squeezed Amaya's shoulder. "To be honest, I'm proud to be someone who cares more than a little for the humans, and I'm guessing that you feel the same."

"Oh, yes, I really do. Which is why this has to be stopped, before it gets worse. Before the entire city is thrown into chaos and pain. We *must* stop it!"

"Well, I'll do some research on it and watch over your city as best I can. I'll look for non sequiturs, things that don't fit in with the rest. People, perhaps, who don't fit in, either, although I doubt one of them could ever find a way to take on our powers."

"You forget, Rebecca, something very important. The first of our kind, Morphea, she was a human."

"Oh, *that* silly theory. No, that's not true, not in the least. I've read nothing of that in our scrolls or books."

"I suppose a passed-around story, no matter how old, might seem untrue if it isn't written on ancient paper. Perhaps, though, the story is older than the scrolls themselves."

"No, nothing is older than the scrolls."

They sat quietly for a few moments, nibbling on the food, and then Amaya announced that she needed to leave.

She said her good-byes to Rebecca and Cillian, both of them assuring her that they would continue looking into her city's problem. Then down the steps she went, toward the walkway that held the castle's traveling mirrors to everywhere in the kingdom.

One thing stayed in Amaya's mind, though, as she walked past each pair of mirrors. What was this power that Rebecca had mentioned? Rebecca had seemed certain that it wasn't a power for good. What if she was wrong, though? What if the power came from something—or even some*one*—that could save the entire city? But that was a silly thought, so she pushed it out of her mind, deciding to just concentrate on getting home as quickly as possible. With a problem this serious, after all, she didn't have any time to waste.

Chapter Eleven

When Isa opened the door to her apartment, her eyes were immediately drawn to her couch, which Martin was sitting on.

"Why aren't you gone yet?" she said. "And why is all your stuff still here?"

"Well, babe—"

"Don't fucking call me 'babe.' You should know better than that. And if your squatting here until I got home is some kind of misguided attempt to worm your way back in here, and back into my life, you've got another think coming. Now, go ahead and pack up what you're going to need in the immediate future. The rest we can deal with later. Maybe I'll even mail it to you, just so I don't have to see you again."

"But…" Martin was clearly trying to come up with some kind of reason they should stay together, why they should work it out…why he should still live in the apartment rent free, perhaps, too. Like *that's* going to happen, she thought.

"Look, we aren't getting back together. I already have a date lined up for tonight, that's how serious I am about this. Get your stuff and get out. I'll be in our—*my*—kitchen." Douchebag, she silently added. Right before she left the room, though, she paused, and told him to leave his keys on the kitchen table. He looked like he wanted to argue, but then he pouted and walked out of the room and into what was now her bedroom—no longer "theirs" either.

Only two nights ago, she and Martin had been sharing the whole place, and it was finally hitting her that they were over. And considering how it had ended, what the very large final straw had been, it seemed like a very good thing that she wouldn't be seeing much more of him.

Isa was, perhaps unsurprisingly, feeling rather happy that the date she was going on tonight was with a woman, and not yet another man. She'd been with men all her life, every single relationship, and now she wondered how much she'd been missing.

She'd almost always liked women more than men. Overly masculine traits usually soured her stomach a little. Men had just seemed like the only option for all those years; she hadn't really spent much time around gay people. But then she'd moved here and started going to Vivian's café. And now her friend wasn't the only one leaning entirely toward the womenfolk. What would Vivian think if she told her, though?

And then there was her family. What would her father think? Her mother would have been fine with it, probably, but she'd died about five years ago, and thoughts of her still stung like crazy. Isa still talked to her sometimes, like her mom was sitting right beside her, but of course, it wasn't at all the same. Her dad was another story entirely. He was a Republican, latently racist, and certainly homophobic, which had become crystal clear when Isa's distant cousin came to visit for a week. That week had turned into three days, as her cousin Kenny had quickly gotten the picture that her father didn't want a "fag" staying under his roof. She'd only been twelve and had cried as Kenny left. She told him through her tears that she didn't feel the same way her dad did, and was still crying as he tossed his suitcase into the backseat of his rental car, only moments from driving off.

"I know, gorgeous girl, I know, and let's hope you and your father never need to come head-to-head about this matter." He'd tipped his fedora at Isa and gotten into the car, driving off into the early morning in a cloud of dust. She hadn't seen or heard from him since. And as to how her father would most likely react? Most likely, if she came out, told him she was gay, it would ruin their already-shaky relationship.

But did she even have a reason to come out? She hadn't slept with a woman outside of her dreams, or kissed one in real life. Tonight would hopefully hold at least some answers to the things she had been thinking about these past few days.

An idea popped into her head—maybe she could get some advice from Vivian. She usually had someone else working the counter this time of the week, so maybe she could help a fellow lesbian out. Not that Isa necessarily qualified as a lesbian, at least not yet. But after tonight...who knew. She thought back to her past sexual escapades. Had she really enjoyed the sex she'd had with men? Yes, at least mostly. But she'd felt like something was missing, she realized. Something like a woman's body, perhaps?

She was still deep in thought when Martin came into the kitchen, two duffel bags slung over his shoulder. "Any chance we can talk about this, ba...Isa?"

"No. You can come back tomorrow to get more stuff, since you obviously weren't prepared to pick it up today. Maybe you should bring a friend. Like Patricia." Isa couldn't help adding that last sentence, that last barb to prick *this* prick's skin.

"I don't think...I mean...um," Martin mumbled, obviously flustered. *Well, good, serves the dickhead, motherfucking bastard right.* Then he continued, his voice low and...sad? "I guess none of the furniture goes to me, because—"

"Yeah, because it was never yours. You obviously get all your things—clothes, toiletries, video games, X-Box, books, all that stuff. And that shitty coffeemaker in the corner. All the rest is mine, as you well know." She smiled as she finished speaking. "Oh, and I'll be here to let you in, so go ahead and leave your key with me."

"Babe…Isa…can't we please try to fix things? I…love you." He had a sad puppy-dog look on his face. Isa half expected him to start whining.

"No, we can't." And his hesitation before he told Isa he loved her implied that he probably no longer did. He probably loved the free rent, the free food, the free cable, Isa thought. *That* stuff he loved, of course. But did he love her? No, probably not. At least not any more.

The look on his face, though, as he put the key on the table, as he glanced over his shoulder in the kitchen doorway, that look almost seemed to say that he had some remaining feelings of affection. She was surprised, but she was feeling just a little sorry for the guy. Yeah, he'd screwed everything up, but he seemed at least a little remorseful, a little regretful. Maybe this would be the push needed to get him back on track in his life.

After she heard the front door shut behind him, she stood up, walking over to the door and leaning against it for a few moments. This was the end of one part of her life and the beginning of the next. She would have to get ready for her date in a few hours, but first, she needed a nap. Or maybe she *wanted* one. Because maybe Lilith would be there as she slept, there to touch her and pleasure her and cheer her up.

But it wasn't Lilith who greeted her in her dreams.

❖

Isa was walking down a dimly lit hotel hallway. Every foot or so a seashell-shaped wall sconce glowed with a gentle, golden light. A door to her left caught her eye—room sixty-nine. Did

Lilith await her beyond the door? There was, of course, only one way to find out.

Inside the room, candles burned on every surface, a much more pleasant glow than the artificial light behind her. "Come in," said a woman, lounging on a large, circular bed right inside the door—a woman who happened to be Ming. "Come in, and help yourself to anything you want."

After walking a few steps toward the bed, and toward Ming, she saw that this wasn't actually a small room like she'd expect in a hotel. No, it was expansive, full of beds, couches, and tables. And beautiful, naked women. When Ming had said, "Help yourself," she couldn't have been referring to the *women*...could she?

"Yes, you may help yourself to any of us you wish. Or, of course, you could choose to come directly to me. It's up to you." Ming moistened her lips, her tongue almost drawing Isa to her.

But instead, Isa decided to go down the stairs. "I...think I'll explore a little, if you don't mind, Ming."

"No, not at all. Explore away. Indulge away. But I would be delighted if you managed to find your way back to me once you've had your fill of the other ladies scattered about this room. I'm who you came here for, after all, and it would be disappointing if you and I didn't get to enjoy each other...didn't get to *taste* each other."

Isa was suddenly very, very wet, and moments after noticing that, she noticed that she was now completely naked. But none of the women were clothed either, so she certainly wasn't out of place.

She decided to follow Ming's suggestion, so she walked farther into the room, past Ming and her bed, and down some wide, carpeted stairs. On the floor, women were draped over couches, over beds, over each other. It was the hottest thing she'd ever seen.

At the bottom of the stairs, she thought of Ming telling her to help herself to anything she wanted. So she did.

The first woman she saw who wasn't with anyone else, who was only fucking herself with a dildo, was the one she approached, ready to offer herself...or maybe, the woman would be the one who became an offering? Isa wasn't sure if she was appealing enough for one of these absolutely beautiful women to want to dally with her, to want to touch, taste, or fuck her.

But this woman certainly did, turning languid, golden eyes toward her. "Can I have you? Because I want you," she purred, and Isa couldn't stop herself. She nodded in assent.

"Yes, I'm all yours." Isa was surprised when those words came out of her mouth, but she was even more surprised when this woman yanked her to her bed. And then, without a moment's warning, her fingers were inside Isa's cunt.

And her fingers certainly hadn't had to fight their way in, because Isa was dripping wet. The woman now slid in a second finger, two fingers fucking Isa's cunt—the way a dick might, she thought, only better. They had more control than a man's dick, and Isa had heard once that lesbians thought of their hands as a woman's version of a cock. Oh, she could certainly see why now, but the way they felt, curving up into her, touching places she hadn't even known she'd had, well, that was miles beyond anything she'd ever felt with a man. No, it was no question which team she wanted to bat for, no question which team she wanted to fuck.

The woman's two fingers had now turned to three, almost without Isa noticing, but she certainly noticed how full she was starting to feel. All of the woman's fingers were curved toward Isa's stomach now, all of them hitting the inside of her cunt in just the right way. Then she started filling up, like something was building inside her, wanting desperately to be released. And then the pressure built up so much Isa almost couldn't hold it back any longer.

"Oh, are you going to come, baby? You gonna come for me?" Isa looked down and saw the woman's grinning face, and those words and her smile were all it took to push Isa, screaming, over that final peak. And as she did, something happened that had never happened before. She came all over the woman's face, ejaculating on her lips, her cheeks, her chin.

Isa collapsed onto the couch, and then her partner crawled up Isa's body, her face only a few inches away from Isa's. "Here, sweetheart, I want you to taste yourself. I want you to taste how delicious you are." She pressed her lips to Isa's in a messy, sticky kiss. And yes, Isa realized, she *did* taste good—sweet, fresh, like nectar. She sighed into the woman's mouth, relaxing into her touch, her kiss, too, and then the woman slipped her tongue into Isa's mouth.

It was Isa's very first kiss from a woman. And this woman was so much better at it than all the men Isa had kissed—gentle, yet firm, and her lips incredibly soft. Soon, Isa was kissing her back, their previously gentle kissing turning hungry and rough, obscene, as the woman grasped each of Isa's breasts, squeezed them, twisted them. Isa hadn't done even the slightest kinky thing before, and now she had just ejaculated, and she was letting these delicate hands attack her breasts. It never got to be too much, though, because every second of it felt surprisingly good. And then she was coming again, coming in waves, her passive body yielding to the woman above her in every way possible.

"Good girl," she whispered into Isa's ear, and those mere words made her come again.

The woman pushed herself up a few moments later and stood, then gestured toward the top of the stairs. "She's waiting for you," she said.

Isa looked up, and there stood Ming, running her fingers through her short, lustrous hair, looking at Isa like she owned her. And maybe she did, if only for this moment, because something was making Isa want to give in, to give all of herself to Ming, and so she waded back toward the stairs, through the writhing, moaning women, pausing to look every now and then. Some were finger-fucking each other, some were masturbating on their own with dildos or fingers, some had fingers or strap-ons shoved into other women's asses. *Hmmm, maybe something to try sometime.*

And then she was going up the stairs, slowly, and Isa stared at Ming as she sashayed back to the bed, swaying her delicate hips and perfect ass. Isa followed her over to the bed, followed her onto it, and said, simply, "Do whatever you want to me."

"Music to my ears, my darling."

Darling…hadn't someone else once called Isa that? She puzzled over that thought, staring up at Ming, staring into her glowing, golden eyes. But Isa couldn't remember, not right now, at least, because all she could think about was how turned on she was, and how much she was looking forward to whatever Ming was planning to do to her.

"So, I can do whatever I want, huh?" Ming began to run a finger down Isa's side, slowly switching from fingertip to fingernail. The switch to something sharper made Isa gasp, and her body tightened and tensed. "If I wanted, I could tie you up and flog you?"

"Yes." That was the only answer Isa could give.

"I could have all those women down there take their turn fucking your pussy, each of them ramming it into you, till you're sore, till you can barely take one…more…dick?" And then Ming slapped Isa's face. The sudden impact shocked her, but more than that, it turned her on.

"Yes, you could," Isa answered, the sting caused by Ming's hand beginning to recede, but not very quickly, and the gush of wetness and heat it had caused wasn't going to recede very quickly either.

And then, as Ming lowered her fingers to Isa's clit, Isa still couldn't help staring into the woman's beautiful gold eyes. They were the most beautiful eyes she'd ever seen, and so Isa told her.

"Thank...thank you, darling." For some reason, Ming seemed a little flustered at the compliment. With eyes like that, she must have received comment after comment, and Isa thought those compliments should probably have gotten old by now—something told her they had. But that same something told her that when she told Ming how beautiful they were, Ming appreciated the oft-repeated words for the first time in years.

"Now, I want to thank you for your kind words," Ming said, her voice softer now, and Isa watched those beautiful eyes get moist, watched her wipe away a tear.

"What's wrong, Ming?"

"Nothing, nothing that cannot be fixed. I just...I just wish our time together could last forever. I wish...I wish things could be different." She smiled then, a sad smile, but before Isa could try to cheer her up, Ming kissed her.

Her kiss held things the other woman's kiss hadn't, things that Isa knew she would miss were they never to kiss again. Ming tasted like summer, like things growing ripe and full on the vine, like sweet berries and sweeter honey. She tasted of other things, too, and Isa noticed more and more each time they kissed—cinnamon, cloves, the freedom of running through a wide-open field in the bright, glowing sunshine. And though Ming's fingers had been stroking Isa's clit, Isa was certain her orgasm came from Ming's kiss, and Ming's kiss alone. Because fuck, was it ever an amazing one—full of passion, wetness, arousal, and it came with a clear, loud sign that Ming wanted her, that she wanted her so, so badly.

Isa pulled back from her, looking into those gorgeous eyes, and saw that Ming was now smiling. A sad smile, though this time it looked a little brighter, a little fuller of cheer. Ming's smile held something else, too, something mysterious, something Isa couldn't quite put into words, but she felt a warmth within herself, looking at that smile, a warmth entirely separate from her arousal.

"You're so very lovely," Isa told her.

Then Ming's smile went away completely. "Yes, you find Ming attractive, don't you?"

"Ming? You mean *you*? Yes, of course. I wouldn't want to go out on a date with you otherwise."

"Wake up then, darling, wake up. You need to get ready for your date, and you shouldn't waste any more time here with me." She kissed Isa on the forehead, a soft press of her lips, and the warmth that had been building in Isa came shooting out of her as she came again.

CHAPTER TWELVE

I sa woke up from the dream feeling confused. Confused, and also incredibly turned on. Well, now the date tonight would be a little weird. But why had she dreamt of Ming, and not Lilith? And why had Ming had golden eyes in the dream, just like Lilith's? Maybe Isa had seen Lilith after all?

A glance at her watch told her she had about one-and-a-half hours before the date, before the date that was making her more nervous by the second. So she decided to call Vivian, hoping that she could give her some advice and potentially help banish some of her first-lesbian-date jitters.

Vivian answered on the second ring. "Hello?"

"Hey, Viv, it's Isa."

"Hi! What's up?"

"I...I...I'm going on a first date tonight."

"Did you break up with Martin?"

"Yes, and it doesn't seem like a mistake."

"Oh, I certainly doubt it is. So, why are you calling me? Is there some problem with the date?"

"It's...different than all my other first dates."

"Oh, is it with a monkey? A circus freak? A—"

"It's with a woman."

"Oh, my, girlie! Welcome to the team! Come right on over, and I'll give you all the tips you want."

"Thanks, Viv. I'll be about fifteen minutes."

Isa slipped on her shoes and grabbed her keys. Hopefully, Vivian could get rid of all of her worries. Or at least *some* of them.

Vivian lived right near Isa, next door to her café, so it was a very short walk. She knocked on the front door of Vivian's bright-yellow house, and Vivian took only a few seconds before she threw open the front door, all smiles. She seemed really excited, and Isa couldn't blame her. After all, they didn't have any other gay neighbors, at least that Isa knew of, so now Vivian was finally getting one. But Isa still wasn't certain—was she really gay? Well, that would most likely be crystal clear by the end of the night.

Vivian and Isa talked for quite a while. Mostly, Vivian quizzed Isa on how her mind had changed toward men—*and* toward *women.* Isa hemmed and hawed at first, then finally gave in and told her.

"I've been having these…dreams, you know."

"Sex dreams?" They were sitting on Vivian's couch, and she leaned forward as Isa told her this, obviously intrigued.

"Yeah, sex dreams. And various people are in them, usually. I've dreamt about this one woman three times, though, and God, is she ever gorgeous. And the dreams are really…doing it for me. So that's why I went exploring in our gay neighborhood, and that's where I met Ming."

"Wow, this dream woman must have some kind of effect on you, for you to switch teams so quickly."

"Yeah, I guess she does. Her name is Lilith, and she's amazing in bed. She's okay out of it, too. And there's this other thing."

Isa was just about to tell Vivian about the book, but just when her friend said, "Yes?" Isa realized how crazy it would sound, and how crazy it would *make* her sound. No, there was no way she could tell Vivian so she'd believe any of it. There was no way Isa wouldn't sound completely and utterly insane.

Instead, she said, "It's just…I'm kind of nervous about the date."

"Well, as long as you don't let Ming U-Haul you, you'll be fine."

"U-Haul me?" What on earth could *that* mean?

"It means that she'll try to come by your place with a U-Haul, try to move in by the second date. It's a dyke thing. Not super common, but still happens sometimes. Happened to me about five years ago, actually. So," she said, standing up and walking Isa to the door, "have fun, and remember, sometimes Saran Wrap can be a lesbian's best friend."

"Saran Wrap?" But Vivian just ushered Isa out of her house with a laugh.

"You'll learn soon enough. Good luck!"

Isa walked home and changed into a flowered knee-length dress and strappy sandals. She checked herself out in the mirror one last time before she left, then went downstairs for the third time that day. This time, though, she was heading into completely uncharted territory.

About twenty minutes later, Isa arrived at the restaurant. She had opted to walk, hoping to possibly work off some of her nerves. Ming was waiting outside, wearing a pale-blue button-down shirt, tucked into creased, classy, slate-colored slacks. She looked good, and so Isa told her, "You look nice."

Ming smiled shyly. "So do you. Shall we go in?"

"Yeah, I'm pretty hungry." But right after saying that, Isa flashed back to her dream. The one with Ming naked. The one where she fucked Isa. Oh, *hell*, Isa thought. Tonight was going to be…interesting.

Ming opened the door of the restaurant for Isa, an act of chivalry Isa had rarely experienced with men. She hadn't realized it at the café where she'd met Ming, but Ming seemed to be on the "butch" side of the spectrum, despite her delicate beauty. Isa realized then that she really still had a ton to learn about women, or at least a lot to learn about the ones who might be attracted to her.

Once they were inside, a woman showed them to a table, then brought them water. Isa took a gulp of hers as a naked Ming appeared in her head again and swallowed it too fast, bringing on a coughing fit. Ming looked concerned, but Isa waved a hand at her to show Ming she was okay.

"You seem…nervous. Has it been a while since you've been on a first date?" Ming asked.

"Yeah, I was in a long-term relationship. Then he cheated on me."

"That's how my last relationship ended, too. She was a real piece of work. But I'd rather not talk about stuff like that. What do you do for a living?"

After they'd ordered, and their food had arrived, Isa learned all about Ming. She worked as a graphic designer at a design firm near the center of the city and was hoping to advance up the ladder there, but had to hide her orientation because it wasn't a comfortable environment for out people, especially for out men. One man there had been gay and out of the closet, and he'd been given worse and worse treatment, until management figured out a way to fire him. So Ming had kept her attraction to women under wraps.

She also told Isa she was a third-generation American, although she could still read Chinese, having taken classes during college. And someday she wanted to make it there, to China, and learn about her history. Shortly after saying this, Ming asked Isa if she had seen the latest art exhibit down the street from the restaurant.

"Yeah, I have. I loved it, I really did."

"My friend Iriana Preston is the artist."

"Oh! How cool!" And then Isa surprised herself by asking, "Any chance I could meet her?"

Ming took a bite of her *masala dosa*. "I bet you could. Maybe she could show you her studio. She has more paintings of that redheaded woman. Says she used to dream about her every now and again."

Isa almost choked on her bite of *naan*. "Yeah, maybe you could arrange it, maybe sometime soon."

"I'd love to. How about this weekend? We could have brunch and then I could take you by her loft. It's huge. I'm so jealous!"

"I've never really been big on lofts. They don't offer enough privacy if you're living with someone else."

"Who needs privacy when you're living with someone you love?" Ming stared off into space for a moment, a dreamy look on her face. "I would want to spend every waking second with the girl of my dreams."

The thought of so little alone time made Isa a bit uncomfortable. She did want to spend time with whomever she wound up with, but she'd still need her space, even with the right person. So maybe this "woman of my dreams" Ming had spoken of wouldn't be her.

Still, after the check had arrived and Ming had insisted on paying it, Isa went ahead and invited Ming back to her place for some wine. But that wasn't the only reason she'd invited her date back to her apartment. It was time to find out, once and for all, whether she liked kissing women outside of her dreams.

Once there, Isa put on some Leonard Cohen and opened a bottle of Riesling. "I hope you don't mind sweeter wines," she said to Ming as she handed her a half-full glass.

"No, I like them just fine, although reds really have my heart." Ming took a sip of the wine and grimaced. "Yep, that's a sweeter wine, all right."

Isa laughed a little. "Sorry, I don't have any red on hand."

"Maybe you can pick some up by the next time I come over. Or maybe I'll bring some by."

Oh my. Was this what Vivian had meant by "U-Haul"? Ming seemed to be moving a little fast for a first date, at least by Isa's standards. But all thoughts of how anything at all was moving left Isa's head as Ming put down her glass and leaned toward her, stopping with her lips just inches away.

"May I kiss you, Isa?" Her voice was breathy, like she was already turned on, even though they hadn't even touched each other yet. That was *so* hot.

And the answer was yes, Isa realized, as she told Ming she could kiss her. Yes, women were just as much of a turn-on in reality as they were in her dreams.

She realized it even more as Ming's lips met hers, lips that were soft and plush, gentle, not like those of a man at all. Ming's kisses were different, too. They were just as full of passion, but this was a slow-moving passage toward sex, one that said time was not important, that she and Ming could take as long as they wanted before either of them started to take off their clothes.

But Isa wasn't ready to take them off, not yet, so she pulled back from Ming after a few moments, something that was surprisingly hard for her to do. "I'm sorry, but can we take it slow?"

Ming cleared her throat. "Sure. I thought…I mean, sure we can. Should we call it a night, then? My vibrator is calling out to me after a make-out session like that."

Isa had started to blush a little, but she still laughed at Ming's joke. "Yeah, I think mine is, too."

"Well, then, I'll give you a call tomorrow, maybe, and we can figure out a good time to get together for brunch and to check out my friend's other artwork. Saturday, maybe?"

"Day after tomorrow? That sounds good to me." Isa scribbled down her number on a piece of paper near the phone. Then she stood up and walked Ming to the front door, and with one more long, sensual kiss, Ming left. God, could the woman ever kiss.

But in her bedroom, making a beeline for her little vibrating friend, Isa was thinking of another kiss, the one she'd had from the "Ming" in her dream earlier that day. The one that was a million times better than the few they'd shared in the real world. And as Isa got out her vibrator and clicked it on, her head filled with a fantasy. Not of Ming, but of a golden-eyed woman with long, red hair—a fantasy of Lilith.

CHAPTER THIRTEEN

Amaya was just about to step through the mirror that led back to her village when she decided she should change her plans. If she went to the Nightmaremakers' village instead, maybe they would have noticed the change she had seen in the city they all brought dreams to. So she took the mirror to the road that led there instead, turning away from the one that led home.

When she reached the Nightmaremakers' village, nestled at the feet of the Tunne Mountains, it was early evening. Two women happened to be standing near where the imposing, wrought-iron gate's entrance to their village lay. Luckily one of them, Shae, was also the village's leader.

"Hello, Shae." Amaya put out her hand. Shae swept some of her always-unruly curls over her shoulder, then took the hand, squeezing it to her chest. She smiled, a slightly dark, but also very suggestive smile. Amaya and Shae had been together before, at least in dreams, so perhaps, Amaya thought, another dream of that sort would be a good idea. It had been a while since she'd entered anyone's dreams in her own world, after all, and she drew great power from those experiences.

"Will you be staying the night?" Shae asked. It was rather obvious what she was thinking, saying such a thing, and Amaya decided that yes, she wouldn't mind joining Shae in her bed, or at least her bed in her dreams.

"I suppose I would like that," Amaya said, a slight smile spreading across her lips. "Yes, that sounds like a very good idea. But before we bed down for the night, I'd love some food, and I need to ask you about something."

"Certainly. Dinner should be ready in about an hour. You and I can use that time to talk."

Once they'd settled onto a plush couch in Shae's living room, Amaya told Shae about what she'd noticed in their shared city. Sadly, Shae didn't have any information, nor had she seen anything like what Amaya spoke of—a great disappointment, but not entirely unexpected.

"I'd have thought we were the only ones to bring pain to people's dreams, but this seems worse than even what the worst of *us* are capable of," she said once Amaya finished speaking. "I'll keep an eye out now for anything that goes on down there, anything similar to what you've told me. Now, let's enjoy a nice dinner, then I'll show you to your quarters."

The meal was delicious: roast pork, yams cooked with brown sugar and ginger, onions with orange zest and paprika, wonderful red wine, and warm apple tart for dessert. Then Shae bid Amaya good night, although both of them knew this wasn't *really* the end of their time together. Amaya went into her quarters, lay on her bed, and joined Shae in her dreams.

In dreamland, Amaya entered Shae's bedroom. She wore only a lace nightgown, her dark-brown nipples visible through its top, her shaved cunt visible through its skirt. She approached the bed, and Shae pulled her to her breast, kissing her only seconds later.

"It's amazing to have you back in my bed, Amaya. You always were such a good lover, and we Nightmaremakers don't get to enjoy all that many good dreams."

"Well, let me make this a very, very good one," Amaya said, slowly running her fingertips down one of Shae's sides. No clothing separated her hand from Shae's flesh, just bare skin against bare skin. Shae's dark eyes fluttered shut, and she shivered at Amaya's touch, but she was obviously enjoying herself already, because a lovely gasp had accompanied the shivers.

Amaya pushed Shae to the bed, gently but firmly. She wanted Shae to know that she would be in charge during this encounter, that she would control Shae's every move. And she knew that Shae would certainly not mind. Shae had always loved giving up control during their time together, had loved Amaya forcing her to do daring things.

Amaya pulled off her nightgown and tossed it to the floor, then placed her nipple right above Shae's mouth. "Lick it," she ordered, and Shae did just that. Then Shae took the nipple into her mouth, rolling it against her tongue, bringing shivers from Amaya now, shivers greater than Shae's had been. Amaya moaned at the feel of Shae's tongue, the wetness and warmth of her mouth bringing wetness and warmth to Amaya's cunt. Then Amaya pulled back, removing her nipple from Shae's mouth, and moved her body farther up, mounting Shae's face.

"You know what to do, my dear," Amaya said. And Shae did, of course, sticking out her tongue and beginning to flick it across Amaya's clit. In this dream, she had given Shae an extra long tongue, the kind that starred in women's fantasies, and so she wasn't too surprised when Shae licked farther down her slit, fucking her hole with her tongue—quick, greedy thrusts that brought moans from Shae, too, because Amaya had connected their pleasures in this dream. She wanted Shae to come just from eating her out, and as she thought of the possibility, she became even wetter.

Shae pushed her tongue farther back, tonguing the sensitive spot between each of Amaya's openings. She snaked her tongue even farther back, then, tickling Amaya's asshole with the tip of it.

"Oh, you know what you're doing, don't you." Amaya gasped. "Been practicing, have you?"

"Mmm-hmm." Shae moaned against Amaya's cunt. And Amaya was getting surpisingly close to coming, just from the touch of Shae's tongue against her asshole. Could she come, just from that alone?

Yes, came the answer, then "Yes, yes, oh yes, oh fuck!" And there came her orgasm, and Shae's, too, both of them crying out, although Shae's cries were muffled against Amaya's cunt.

❖

Amaya woke from the dream with a start. It felt as though… was someone in the room with her? She glanced around, suddenly nervous. No, no one was there, the room pitch-dark, but with no movement, no breathing. The mirror in the corner showed nothing. She lay back down and prepared to enter Shae's dream again.

❖

He watched the woman on the bed, sleeping quietly. Amaya. Oh, she would be sleeping for quite a while, but not quietly, not for much longer. He slowly approached the bed, stroking the side of her face with the back of his hand once he reached her side. Then, beginning to smile, he turned his hand over and raked his claws across her face, leaving thin white lines. Yes, she wouldn't be waking up any time soon. Not if he and his new friend had any say in it—his new friend who wanted to join him in wreaking havoc in the human world.

When she had discovered him, he'd been ready to strike out, to bring her pain, but when she'd told him she could help him, when she'd offered up her power, his mind had certainly changed. He grinned, sharp-toothed, staring down at the woman. She looked so very helpless, and this delighted him. He almost laughed with glee.

Then, grinning even wider, he turned and walked through the mirror and entered Amaya's dreams.

CHAPTER FOURTEEN

Last night had held another nightmare for Isa. This one had the same creature as always, chasing her, as always. As she ran, mirrors to her right and left showed the same scene—a woman on a bed, her face flecked with droplets of sweat, and Isa had to watch, over and over again, as the woman tossed back and forth, her brow furrowed, her mouth open. And Isa had to listen, too, as horrible sounds of pain and distress escaped the sleeping woman's lips. Isa woke with a gasp of breath, full of fear.

Luckily, this time it was already light out when she woke up. Luckily, because she wouldn't possibly get a single second more sleep. At least she was more awake than she usually was first thing in the morning. But rituals were rituals, so she went into the kitchen and started some coffee brewing. She couldn't help wishing for those goddamn dreams to stop, a fruitless wish that she had made many times by now.

Why couldn't she have dreamt of Lilith instead? Even though those dreams were the only action she was getting at the moment, it certainly wasn't *painful* to have them. Oh, no, it certainly wasn't. And crazy as it seemed, she missed Lilith a little, and her sleep-hungry body led her into her couch and toward Lilith's gift, the Millay book. She brushed her fingers across the cover, then settled onto the couch, flipping through the book and reading a few of the poems.

But none of this, the nightmares or the sex dreams, were in reality, and certain things still were, like rent and bills. So once she had fixed and eaten some oatmeal, she got out her laptop and wrote for as long as she could. The words didn't come as easily as usual, but that was common after a night containing one of her *far*-too-common nightmares.

Five hours and plenty of writing later, the lack of sleep caught up to her. She pulled a blanket over herself and lay down on the couch, just to rest a moment or two.

❖

Isa was back in the hotel room, but this time it contained only a normal-sized room, and this time only Ming was in the room. "You're back in my dreams, huh?" Isa asked her, as she began to walk toward the bed. "Trying to prepare me for my first time with her? Where's Lilith, anyway? I wouldn't mind seeing her instead."

Ming smiled. "Perhaps you can be with both of us." And then Isa watched as Lilith walked through the hotel door, toward the bed, toward her.

"Hi, Lilith. Thank you for the book. I've loved reading it."

"I'm happy to hear you like it. Maybe you'll find another gift once you wake up."

"Really?" Isa smiled at the thought of what might be waiting for her after her dream. The book had been a wonderful choice, so she couldn't help but think that whatever else Lilith came up with would probably be wonderful, too.

"Are you preparing me for my first lesbian sex in real life?" she asked Lilith. "I mean, it seems like you're the one in control of these dreams, unless I'm mistaken."

"Yes, something like that." A look flickered across Lilith's face. Was it a sad look? But soon her expression turned back to one of desire, a desire that seemed to be directed right at Isa. So what could Isa do, then, but follow her to the bed and join her and Ming? Because Lilith certainly wasn't alone in thinking lustful thoughts.

"So, which one of you should I go down on first?" Isa asked. Each woman chuckled a little, their laughs almost entirely the same, if not identical.

"Why don't you go down on Ming while I fuck you?" Lilith suggested, a dildo and harness suddenly appearing on her crotch.

"That sounds terrific." Isa grinned to show exactly how incredibly dirty her current thoughts were.

Ming inched her way up the bed, spreading her legs, revealing a soaking-wet pussy. Isa lowered her face to it and made her back concave, offering her cunt to Lilith. And she took Isa's offering, teasing her hole with her strapped-on dick, and Isa moaned into Ming's cunt as she lowered her lips to it. Isa began to lick Ming's clit, moaning again as Lilith ever so slowly slid the dick inside Isa's pussy.

Lilith began to fuck Isa with her dick then, grabbing her hips, and Isa fought to keep her lips on Ming's cunt. Ming tasted good to Isa, but Isa knew, from the first dream she'd had with Lilith in it, that Lilith tasted far better.

And then Isa felt Lilith's thumb slide its way down her crack, all the way down to her asshole. Lilith pressed it gently against that hole, as she continued to fuck Isa, and then began to slip it inside. Isa knew lube was needed for such things in real life (not that she'd ever done anything like that), but of course you didn't need any in your dreams (or fantasies). And she knew right away that she loved the feel of Lilith's finger inside that hole, loved having Lilith's dick and finger invading each of her holes...oh, did she *ever*.

Isa continued to lick Ming, coming close to getting off, and then there it was, an utterly amazing orgasm, flooding her body with pleasure. She shot up from Ming's cunt, no longer able to care about anyone else's pleasure but her own, and the orgasm took over her every thought, until she collapsed onto Ming, completely sated.

"Wake up now, my darling," Isa heard Lilith say. "And enjoy my gift. It is given with…it is given freely."

❖

The room seemed brighter than when Isa had fallen asleep, which seemed rather strange. It should have been darker. Isa pushed herself up to a sitting position and realized why it was so much brighter: a vase sat to her left, pale-blue glass with what looked like opals and moonstones set into its rim. And inside the vase were flowers that glowed, that put off their own light. They were the flowers Lilith had shown her a few nights back in her dream in the bar.

"Fuck me!" Isa yelped. Maybe Lilith would take that statement as a suggestion, but Isa didn't mean it that way. No, it just expressed her pure, undiluted shock of seeing those flowers *from* her *dream*, sitting on the table beside her couch. *How is this possible?*

However, in terms of things that were "possible," the book Lilith had given her earlier certainly wasn't either. And the flowers were absolutely beautiful, admittedly, like nothing Isa had seen before, their blue glow illuminating the room in a most amazing way. She stroked one gently. No way would she believe they were really there until she'd touched them.

But there they were, the flower petals soft against her hand, and so Isa picked up the vase and carried it into her bedroom, placing it on her bedside table. Light to read by that night, perhaps.

She went back into the living room, shaking a little. But, strangely enough, she felt happiness, too. It was certainly a lovely gift, even lovelier than the book. Things were getting weirder and weirder. But did she mind it? Did she? No. She really didn't.

It seemed impossible for Lilith to enter her reality, Isa thought, as she sat back down on the couch, or Lilith would have done it by now. Would Isa welcome her into her reality, if she could? She didn't know for sure, but she thought, a little sadly, that she would most likely never have to make up her mind about it. And that answered her question well enough.

Then her phone rang, startling her out of her reverie. *Of course.* Ming had said she would call today. So Isa picked it up and answered it, hearing exactly the person she'd expected.

"Hi, Isa, it's Ming. How are you?"

"Not bad." She picked up a pen and began to doodle on the pad of paper near the phone. "You?"

"Pretty good, actually. Especially after our date last night. I had a lovely time."

And I had a lovely time eating you out in my dream while Lilith fucked me. "Me, too. So, we were thinking of getting together again tomorrow? Is that still good for you?"

"It's great, yeah. How about I pick you up at eleven? We can go to brunch at a really great diner near my friend's place, then walk to her studio. Does that work for you?"

"Uh-huh. So, see you then?"

"Yes, see you then. Take care."

"Bye."

Well, now Isa had plans the next day. Another date with her real-life love interest. Did she like Ming, though? Maybe. Yes. Not a huge amount, but Ming seemed like a nice-enough person, and Isa had certainly enjoyed kissing her. Not as much as she enjoyed kissing Lilith, though. Which was crazy, she thought, because despite all the proof—the flowers, the book, the note—

Lilith was still just a woman in her dreams. Not meaningful, not really.

Or maybe not, Isa thought, as she looked down at what she'd been sketching. Lilith's face stared up at her from the pad of paper, a slight smile on her lips, looking as beautiful as ever.

Isa stayed in and read that night, watched a little TV, and did some writing. She was falling behind a bit with her required number of blog entries, although her boss hadn't reprimanded her. She'd always turned in more posts than necessary, so maybe said boss was going easy on her because of that. But between her newly realized lesbianism and her dream lady, she wasn't as clear-headed as usual, not even close. Which made writing about everyday stuff very challenging. Admittedly, she'd had a little fun writing about a starlet who had just come out of the closet— good for her!

Isa wasn't even close to ready to come out of hers, though. If there even *was* one to come out of. If there was, it had been constructed without her knowing about it, built up around her in the dead of night while she was fast asleep. Actually, that wasn't so far from the truth, she thought with a small laugh. Lilith had helped her build said closet, as it was certainly beginning to seem like there was one. Ming's kisses on their date had definitely turned Isa on, and she hadn't really paid attention to any of the men on the TV shows she'd been surfing among. No, she'd paid far more attention to the beautiful, scantily clad women on them. For the first time, she wasn't actually bothered by their almost-nudity. No, instead it turned her on and made her wish for her vibrator. Or, better, for an almost-nude (or completely nude) woman of her own.

She went to bed wondering how her date would go the next day. Would brunch lead to more? Some messing around, perhaps? Some nudity? Some sex? She didn't know how fast women usually took these things, but she wanted to follow the three-date rule. The whole difference between how quickly men and women got attached still confused her, and she didn't want to send Ming the wrong message, scare her away by sleeping with her too soon. No, only sex with Ming in Isa's dreams would be allowed for now

Maybe I should make it four dates, Isa thought before she drifted into a deep slumber, awaking in the morning without a single memory of a dream.

CHAPTER FIFTEEN

The sound of Ming's knock on her front door yanked Isa out of the book she'd been reading—one she'd never read before, which had been a gift from Vivian. It was about two women who met as nurses during World War II, and Isa was sobbing when she opened the door.

"Oh, God, Isa! What's wrong?" Ming's brow wrinkled, and she looked incredibly concerned.

"Sally died!" Isa wiped her eyes with her hands, but the tears were still coming strong. "I'm sorry, I just...I didn't mean to answer the door crying."

"Oh, it's fine, really. Is Sally...was she a relative?"

"No, she was a nurse! In World War II! And she and Maryanne can never be together now, because she died saving Maryanne's life!" Isa choked back a few more sobs, the tears slowing a bit, but still not stopping entirely.

"Oh, of *course*. You've been reading one of H. R. Moore's books. *The Nurses*."

"Yes," Isa said, laughing through the tears. "I'm sorry, you must have thought someone I knew...I mean, it's just so sad, you know."

"Yeah, I loved that book. You should read *A Promise Among Liars* next. But I'll warn you, the ending of that one is even more depressing. Maybe a lighter book next instead? I can recommend a few really good queer authors, actually." Ming smiled at her, placing her hand on Isa's shoulder—the lightest touch, but it helped the tears to finally stop flowing. "You still going to be able to join me for brunch? I can postpone if you need to go into mourning or something like that. But my friend Iriana will probably be disappointed. She was looking forward to meeting you."

"No, no, I think I can pull myself together well enough to manage. After all, somehow, Maryanne will find a way to go on. Maybe she'll meet someone back in the States."

"Yes, I bet she will, great woman that she is."

Isa got her purse and went downstairs with Ming. Time for their second date to start.

Ming's car was a black Honda, and the inside was much cleaner than Martin's had been, which came as a delight to Isa. She'd gotten so sick of trying not to let her feet touch the pile of McDonald's wrappers and soda cans that she'd mostly avoided riding in it with him the last year or so. Public transportation had its share of problems, but, unlike Martin's car, you didn't have to worry about accidentally shoving your favorite pair of white-satin heels into a moldy burger. At least, that wasn't *quite* as likely on the bus.

"Your car is so clean!" Isa couldn't help remarking.

"Yeah, my mom trained me to keep it that way. She was always a stickler for tidiness. And Godliness, too, but she's still accepted me as I am. Even is hoping for some grandchildren from me and a partner at some point." She glanced at Isa when they stopped at a light, and Isa wondered if she was gauging her reaction to the idea of kids. *Their* kids, perhaps? At the moment, Isa thought that other people's kids were quite cute most of the time, but she was glad they weren't *her* kids, at least for the time being.

"Yeah, that's a mom thing, all right. Or so I hear, at least."

"What do you mean?"

"My, uh, mom died. About five years ago. Now all I have left is my dad, and he and I aren't really all that close. I don't think...I mean, I'm not out to him. And he would write me out of his life entirely if I did tell him."

"Well, maybe you'd be better off without him in your life, if he won't accept you as you are. And I'm sorry about your mom."

"Thanks. She was, in a word, awesome." Isa stared out her window for a few minutes, lost in thought, and Ming placed her hand on Isa's thigh. It comforted Isa, the feel of her hand resting there gently, and she smiled as Ming squeezed her leg, then turned and looked at Ming's hand, sitting there in such a gentle and reassuring way. Then, almost without thinking, she placed her hand over Ming's.

Isa looked up at Ming then, wondering if Lilith would have done the same thing. Definitely, she decided. Lilith definitely would have. It felt...different with Lilith than it did with Ming, Isa thought, even though she'd only been with Lilith in her dreams, but Ming was real, flesh and blood, and that thought ended any idle speculation of what Lilith would or would not have done.

"Here we are," Ming said, as they pulled into a three-hour parking space. Once out of the car, Ming pumped a bunch of quarters into the meter, then gestured toward a diner to their right. The sign said Minnie's Diner, and it looked charming, either made to look like a train car, or possibly made out of a real one, painted bright red with lime-green trim. Not necessarily a color choice Isa would have gone with, but in this case, it just added to the charm.

"This place looks really great," Isa said as they headed toward the front door.

"And just wait until you try their strawberry and blueberry pancakes. Or pretty much anything else they serve," Ming replied as she opened the door for Isa.

"Thanks."

A waitress led them to a table, where they were given menus and their drink orders were taken. Their waitress's nametag said Ricki, and she had a huge, curly, disaster of red hair (obviously out of a bottle, Isa thought) all around her face. "Disaster" was the only word for it, because there was far too much of it for only one person, and the shade of red was certainly not one seen in nature, unless you were talking about the tropics.

"I like your...hair," Isa told her, and she watched out of the corner of her eye as Ming suppressed a laugh.

"Thank you, darlin'. Just got it done at the hair salon." Ricki looked quite happy at the compliment, so Isa didn't feel bad about the lie. Her mom had trained her to give people compliments whenever she had the chance, and it didn't matter immensely, as she had taught Isa, whether or not you meant it. Like complimenting Ricki's hair, for example.

"You like her hair?" Ming asked quietly as Ricki walked away.

"No, not at all. But I thought she'd like to hear that someone—me—did."

Ming seemed to approve, quickly reaching across the table to put her hand on Isa's.

"They're gay-friendly here?" Isa asked her.

"Well, yes. Couldn't you tell that Ricki is more like a Marcus?"

"Oh. I missed the Adam's apple."

"Well, she's very good with makeup, even if she isn't the best with hair. With the right makeup, you can almost make it disappear."

"'She'? Do you call a drag queen 'she'? I'm not totally filled in on all the rules," Isa told Ming in a slightly embarrassed tone.

"Are you...is this your first time dating a woman?" Ming narrowed her eyes a little, which made Isa worry what would happen if she told Ming the truth.

But she had to, no question about it. "Yes, it is. I'm…my whole being attracted to women, it's kind of a new thing."

"Well, as much as I don't want to be your test case, I like you, Isa, so I guess I'm volunteering. Just don't break my heart, okay? No going back to men if it winds up you don't like being with a woman."

"Of course not." But Isa couldn't promise not to break her heart. No, that was impossible to promise. After all, there was Lilith, and…but, yet again, she had to tell herself how ridiculous the idea of being with a woman from her dreams was. Isa couldn't even touch her, at least not when she was awake. And while Lilith seemed interested in her, there was no real way to tell. Maybe Isa was just someone entertaining, a distraction, a woman Lilith thought was hot and wanted to dote on for the time being. Lilith's words said something different, but you never really knew with these things.

Ricki setting Isa's iced tea and Ming's iced coffee on the table brought Isa back into the room. "What'll you be havin', missies?"

Isa didn't order the pancakes that Ming had suggested. Instead, she told Ricki, "I'd like…the avocado omelet. And could you hold the onions?" After all, if there was going to be any kissing, onion-breath would not add to the experience.

"And for you, ma'am?" Ricki turned to Ming, and then Isa noticed that yes, she *did* have an Adam's apple, albeit one covered with a lot of makeup.

"I'll have the bagel and lox, with a sesame-seed bagel."

Ricki took their menus, then leaned toward Ming, saying softly into her ear, "Nice to see you here with someone, Ming, darlin'."

Ming blushed and looked down at the table, which made Isa want to tell her she was a little happy Ming was here with someone, too. Instead, Isa just squeezed her hand, causing Ming to look up from the table and grin.

Their food arrived not too much later, and in between bites, they talked some about their childhoods. Ming had been born in Texas, but she and her parents and older sister had moved to Isa's city about twenty-five years ago. Ming had been eight when they moved, and that told Isa her age. Ming's parents had only been living in Texas to take care of her grandmother, who had passed away shortly before they moved. Her mom and dad, Arthur and Song, had moved Ming and her sister, Jing, away from there as soon as possible. Chinese people were not at all welcome in their small town, and the townspeople made that more than clear. It made Isa's own childhood, even with her bigoted father, seem a little more comfortable in retrospect.

"So, your parents are okay with you being gay?" Isa asked her as they waited for their check.

"Yeah, totally. I actually knew I was gay by the time I was fourteen, and so, even though I was scared, I came out to them. They both told me that they would love me no matter what, and who *I* loved didn't matter in the least, as long as that person was kind and gentle with me."

"That's so great. I can't really say the same for my dad, but my mom would have been perfectly supportive. She was so lovely…I have no idea what she was doing with my dad. I mean, he was nice enough to her, but they were as different as night and day." Isa looked down for a moment, slightly quirking her lips. "He was night, of course."

Ming chuckled. "I think I get what you mean. My dad could be strict, sometimes, my mom, too, but they're great. Maybe you can meet them someday. I think you'd get along with them really well."

So now I'm supposed to meet her parents? This certainly was moving at a quicker pace than Isa was used to, but did she mind? Ming might have been making up her mind about Isa faster than Isa was making up her mind about her, but there were worse things in a potential partner. It was nice how easily Ming's approval had come so far. But would she approve of Isa's lack of experience in the bedroom? After all, dreams were not reality, and this, whenever "this" happened, would be Isa's first time with a woman. God only knew how it would go.

Ming insisted on paying, and then they left. Ricki winked at them as they went outside, saying, "Have fun, kids."

"She's great," Isa told Ming as they walked toward a large building across the street.

"Yeah, she certainly is. She's been working there as long as I remember, and I've been going there for years upon years." Ming pointed at the building they had just reached. "This is where Iriana lives. You ready to see the rest of her masterpieces?"

"Sure."

Up a few flights of stairs, Ming led Isa up to a door with the number sixteen on the front. The door was painted like "Starry Night," blue and gold and full of life. It was beautiful, but Isa was looking forward to seeing Iriana's original work more. Ming knocked, and a few moments later, a woman with chestnut-brown hair, with touches of silver in it on either side of her face, opened the door. She was wearing a black apron, covered in paint and what looked to be clay, which made it appear that she had been creating something right before Isa and Ming arrived.

"Ming! Hello! Come in, come in," and she opened the door wide.

Iriana's place was amazing, Isa thought. It was on the top floor of the building, and the wall across from the door was actually made up entirely of glass, with large, black drapes bunched up on either side. A kitchen was slightly ahead of them and to their left, what seemed to be her bedroom to their right, and then a number of easels and dozens of paintings and half-finished sculptures and bags of clay scattered across most of the floor. A TV sat right past the kitchen, but it had no screen and was instead filled with a lush, dark-green plant that had pale-yellow, tubular flowers peeking out of the greenery.

"I *love* your place. It's just...wow." Which was pretty much the only way one could respond to such an amazing place. Sometimes inflection had to do what words couldn't.

"Thank you, thank you. I love it, too. Now, can I get either of you something to drink? Maybe an Italian soda? I just picked up some absolutely delicious raspberry syrup, and I could mix it with some of the lime I bought a few weeks ago."

"That sounds great," Isa said, feeling a little distant. She was still taking in Iriana's place and wishing a little that her own place was at least half this nice. But she couldn't possibly afford it on her writer's salary.

"Why don't you two sit down while I mix up the sodas?" Iriana gestured toward a couch across from the kitchen, and so Isa followed Ming over to it and sat down on the part that wasn't covered in huge splotches of paint, Ming doing the same. The splotches looked dry enough, but Isa still didn't want to risk staining her white sundress. It was one of her favorites, after all.

Iriana took a clear bottle out of her fridge, pouring soda water into three slim, tall glasses. Then she added each of the syrups, stirring each mixture with a long-handled spoon after she'd poured a splash of the green and red syrup into each glass. She carried the three glasses over to the table in front of the couch, all of them balanced on an ancient-looking silver tray. The tray had a carving of a sleeping woman on it, lying on a sofa with her eyes shut tight.

"That's a beautiful tray," Isa said.

"It was a gift," And for just a second, Iriana looked sad, but that expression left her face so swiftly that Isa barely had time to register it. And perhaps it had never been there in the first place, as Iriana now looked just as happy as she had when they'd arrived.

"What got you started as an artist?" Isa asked her as she sipped her soda.

Iriana instantly tensed. But luckily, even though it seemed Isa had hit a very sensitive spot, Iriana still was willing to answer her question. "It all began," she said, her tone turning slightly wistful, "with a dream."

A *dream*?

"She came to me often in my dreams, and she was interesting beyond just her looks. They were lovely dreams, and so was she, and so I began painting her, and sculpting her, trying to capture her likeness. And I still do, although the dreams are long gone. They stopped about ten years ago, and I haven't had one since. Which, silly though it may sound, makes me a little sad." She wiped at her eyes, turning away from Ming and Isa for a moment. "Sorry, I'm just tired. I didn't sleep too well last night. Bad dreams."

"Oh, I know how that can be," Isa said, trying not to think of her recent nightmares as she spoke. And she also knew what it was like to dream about a beautiful woman, one who you felt some kind of connection to.

"Would you like to see some of my work?" Iriana looked back toward them now, and her face had become cheerful again.

"I'd love to," Isa told her, placing her now-empty glass back on the tray.

Iriana led her over to the painting closest to them, which was facing away from the couch. It was similar to the ones Isa had seen in the museum, the same woman, her face turned away, with blazing red hair and an amazing body. Luscious, not delicate, not breakable like the ones Isa remembered from magazines and TV. She looked toward Ming at that thought, seriously checking out her body for the first time, and realized then that she certainly wouldn't mind seeing Ming naked, considering her full curves and, Isa thought, great tits. Not a thought she'd really harbored before, at least about a real woman, sitting across a room from her, but yeah, they were great all right, something that was clear to Isa even through Ming's white T-shirt. Heaven forbid she wore something low-cut to one of their dates.

Isa looked back at the painting, appreciating the way Iriana had made the woman's hair look almost touchable, like hair you'd want to run your fingers through for hours. Like Lilith's. But the woman's figure looked different than Lilith's, her hips wider, her butt bigger, and unlike the hair (admittedly, it wasn't quite as lovely, or as intense a color as her dream woman's), it was obviously not Lilith's body. Which of course would make absolutely no sense at all, Isa thought. But many things weren't making sense these days—like the glowing flowers and the Millay book back at her apartment.

Iriana led her around to the rest of her paintings, saying nothing about the woman in them, instead answering Isa's questions about the methods she'd used to get certain effects in them. Isa really knew nothing about painting, so it was all incredibly interesting to her, learning all that Iriana had to tell her about what it took to get light to appear a certain way, or how she used a brush to get hair to look as real as it possibly could. Then Iriana showed her the sculptures, answering her questions about them as well. Was it a relief to Iriana to not be talking about the star of each and every painting, this woman who had bewitched her enough to become her permanent and only muse, to have the honor of appearing in each and every piece of artwork she had ever created?

But how had mere dreams managed to affect Iriana so intensely? And then came a silly thought. Did Iriana's dreams have anything to do with hers?

Isa couldn't possibly have asked her in front of Ming, though, even if she wanted to desperately, so she gave Iriana her number and suggested that the two of them meet again sometime. "Alone" was the unspoken part of that suggestion, and Isa hoped they would be able to get together sometime soon, just the two of them.

Yes, just the two of them. To talk about their dreams…and the women who happened to be in them.

CHAPTER SIXTEEN

When they got back downstairs, a glance at her watch told Isa that it was about half-past three. The sky was slightly hazy, but rain seemed unlikely, so when Ming suggested they go to her favorite used-clothing store, Isa took her up on the offer. It wound up having a really great selection, and she and Ming had a great time trying to each find the most hideous thing in the store. Ming ended up buying a pair of black ballet flats, and Isa discovered an awesome pair of Jackie O-style sunglasses and a black trench coat in perfect condition.

Then they went down the street a little and came across a grocery store Ming really liked. Penny's Market had an amazing variety of fruit and vegetables, as well as a huge section of things Isa hadn't even known existed before then, such as a dahlia-like yellow-orange fruit that was apparently called Buddha's Hand.

Isa bought a jar of mixed Spanish olives, and then, when Ming pointed out that it was almost dinnertime, Isa agreed to join her over at her place for a meal. Ming selected a number of fresh ingredients for a salad and got a jar of pesto, some whole-wheat pasta, and sun-dried tomatoes preserved in olive oil.

They put the groceries into Ming's car and headed off—her home was about a fifteen-minute drive from the grocery store. She lived in a slightly suburb-like area, but the houses weren't all the same, all of them various sizes and colors. Ming's was forest green and rather small, but sweet looking, Isa thought, with white trim around the roof. It also had, as well as a lovely, healthy-looking lawn, a lawn gnome and a few plastic flamingos out front. "What can I say, I like kitsch," Ming told Isa as she watched her take them in.

"Me too," Isa told her, although that was only somewhat true.

"Do they have names?" she asked Ming as she unlocked the front door. If they did, maybe the names would be interesting ones…and Isa was guessing that maybe the type of person to have lawn gnomes and flamingos on their front lawn would also be the type who might name them.

"The gnome is Alfred, and the flamingos are Tick and Tock. The three of them don't get along very well, and I have to reprimand them from time to time. Especially Alfred. He's a real bastard."

"Great names," Isa said with a laugh. The great names—and the "life" Ming had given to her lawn decorations—were two more things to perhaps add to her interest in Ming.

After putting the bags on the black-and-white-checkered counter, Ming got some water boiling, then went over to a stereo in the corner of her *entirely* black-and-white kitchen (even the appliances were either black or white), and put on some music. Ella Fitzgerald starting singing in her rich, deep voice, and Isa told her, "I like Ella a lot. She's perfect music to cook to."

"To kiss to, as well," Ming said, and she walked up to Isa and closed the distance between them, kissing her hard and fast right as Ella hit an especially high note.

Just like last time, her kisses turned Isa on an amazing amount—so much that she didn't mind when Ming ushered her into the bedroom and asked Isa if she could take off her clothes. So much that Isa didn't hesitate in telling her yes.

Ming was a very different lover than Lilith, different than the dream version of her as well, in that she took her time, undressing Isa very slowly. But soon enough, Isa was down to just her underwear. And even though she hadn't been planning to sleep with Ming on this date, she had still decided to wear some of her nicer lingerie. This set had black lace over pale-pink silk and consisted of a demi-bra and some incredibly small panties.

And Ming seemed to approve. "Wow, your underwear is fucking amazing, Isa. So hot. So, so hot. Just like you." She bent down to her knees, kissing Isa through the panties, tonguing her in just the right place to make Isa squirm and sigh. She practically melted onto the floor, and the bed behind her, pressed up against her knees, was the only thing that kept her upright. And then she was upright no longer, Ming having pushed her onto the bed, and then Ming unhooked Isa's bra with none of the struggle men seemed to always have when doing the same. Only someone who takes off her own bra, day in and day out, would be able to do the act of taking a bra off such extreme justice, Isa thought. Ming slowly slid each strap down each arm, kissing Isa right above where each strap had just been as she eased it down.

This was Isa's first time being topless with a woman, at least when the woman was allowed to touch her breasts. Her first time outside of dreams, of course. Her third time with Ming, too, although it hadn't been her—the real flesh-and-blood her—until now. And was there *ever* a difference. Not that the dreams didn't feel amazing, but something about having a real woman's hands on her skin, a real woman's fingers gently rolling her nipples back and forth, then pinching them, *just* a little, did unimaginable things to Isa. Things that made her very, very wet, things that made her clit begin to throb, which had never happened with a man, Isa realized.

Then Ming took one of Isa's nipples into her mouth, making it warm and wet. Which heated Isa up even further than before, until she was practically ready to beg Ming to tear off her panties. Isa wanted Ming to move her lips down farther, until they rested on her sweetest of spots—her rock-hard, throbbing clit. Isa knew she'd soaked through her panties by then, could feel how incredibly wet they were in the spot between her thighs, and so of course she had no need to be wearing anything down there anymore.

Then Ming gently brushed her fingers between Isa's legs. "How did you manage to get so wet, so quickly?" She pushed herself up until her face was right above Isa's.

"This is…you probably kinda realized this…but this is my first time with a woman." In real life, at least. "And it's turning me on a whole fucking lot more than I could have possibly imagined."

"Oh, so this does it for you more than being with a man? Well, phew, isn't that a relief!" Ming grinned at her, then, in one swift movement, off went Isa's panties and on went Ming's mouth.

"Oh fuck!" Those were the only words Isa could manage for the rest of the time Ming went down on her, Ming's tongue bringing her over the edge over and over…and over again. This was Isa's first time having multiple orgasms, and she kinda liked them, liked them a *lot*.

Finally, Isa had to stutter, "Too much…stop…please." She was finally over-sensitized; she had finally had too much.

Ming raised up her face, her smile wide.

"You're…proud of yourself, aren't you?" Isa said. Her voice sounded the same way it had sounded the few times she'd smoked pot. She sounded airy, and possibly a bit dumbfounded. But this was a much better reason for her voice to be altered in such a way.

"Of course I'm proud!" Ming answered. "I didn't…I mean, you're really, really orgasmic. Is that…" She paused, crawling up the bed to lie beside Isa. "Is that only with me?"

"Yeah. I've never…that's never happened before." Isa sighed as she noticed how limp her body was, and then she smiled a goofy smile.

"Well, I'm damn proud of myself, then." Ming kissed Isa on the cheek. "Now, how about some dinner?"

Dinner was great, Isa thought, although the conversation didn't flow as well as it had up until then. It might have been that she was still processing the fact that she'd now finally had sex with a woman and, further, that she'd had sex with a woman and enjoyed it. A lot. Isa recalled Vivian telling her that, from her limited experience with men, women just did "it" better. And hell, she was *so* right.

They didn't have sex again that night, although Ming did talk Isa into sleeping over. A part of Isa wanted to sleep in her own bed, though. She'd never done well on sleepovers at boyfriends' homes, always having to stop herself from endlessly tossing and turning. And worse, she'd usually have one of her nightmares once she fell asleep.

But it turned out that having female energy with her in the bed was different. Soothing, comforting, or maybe something else, but what it came down to was that she had a great night's sleep. She even fell asleep in mere moments, Ming's body pressed up against hers, only the smallest layers of cloth between their bodies. She had loaned Isa a slip-like nightgown, while Ming slept in panties and a T-shirt, a look that definitely worked for her, in Isa's opinion. She almost wanted to have sex again, but… would she have to eat Ming out this time? Isa was quite nervous about the prospect. Maybe in the morning, though, she would try eating pussy for the very first time. What was the worst that could happen, after all?

It wasn't the very first time, though. No, the very first time, at least in an alternate reality, had been in her dreams, in that first dream of Lilith, where Isa had eaten her out, and it'd seemed she'd done quite a good job. If only it would be that easy in real life. Maybe it would, but she would just have to work up her nerve and do it, whether Ming asked her to or not. It seemed the fair, right thing to do, Isa thought, and who knew—maybe she would do a great job after all.

CHAPTER SEVENTEEN

No going down on Ming was required the next morning, as instead she went down on Isa again. The orgasms were not plural this time, just a single rather good one. Isa did work up the nerve to offer, but Ming said it was fine, that there'd be plenty of time for her to return the favor.

"Right now, I just want to get the idea across that women are a million times better in bed. I should know. I did some time in the 'man trenches' just to check."

Isa laughed at the thought—like men were something you had to suffer through until you realized how glorious women could be. Well, she'd put in her own time in said trenches and had gained nothing worthwhile from it—just a few broken hearts and some lockjaw. Hopefully she wouldn't have some similar ailment caused by converting to eating pussy. She made a mental note to ask Vivian about that.

Breakfast was fruit salad and Greek yogurt, both bought at the grocery store the evening before. Had Ming planned this? Well, it didn't really matter if she had. Isa had enjoyed herself, and that was all that mattered.

She decided to catch the bus home later that morning and told Ming as she left her house that she'd had a lovely time. They stood on Ming's porch as she kissed Isa good-bye, but as she did, she heard a grouchy *harrumph* of displeasure from behind them.

Isa began to turn her head in the direction it had come from, but Ming cupped her jaw and turned Isa's head back toward her face. "That's just my neighbor. She hates any sort of PDA, but she's sweet enough, other than that. Makes the same noise over the straight couples, too, and she's baked me cookies a few times."

So Isa turned toward the street and smiled and waved, which brought another *harrumph* from the petite old lady with short, bluish hair and a yellow, zipped-up robe. She shook the newspaper she was holding at Ming and Isa and said, "You young people, always with your kissing in public. Get a room, you two. Get a room." Isa watched as she shuffled back toward her front door, feeling thankful that the woman wasn't offended by the fact that she and Ming shared a gender. Luckily, just their PDA had caused those *harrumphs*. Isa knew she had plenty of time to feel the insult of homophobia later, but she was just glad she hadn't experienced any of it yet.

Then again, Isa thought, heading down the street, she'd only been attracted to women for a very short time, and had been sleeping with a real live one for an even shorter length of time. She hadn't had to deal with a lot of the stuff that Ming and Vivian probably had. Going to high school gay, for one thing. Or whatever her dad might have done to her if he'd known she was gay while she was still under his roof. Her mom might have had something to say about it, but Isa very well could have ended up homeless.

She thought about this new aspect of her life as she walked the three blocks toward the bus stop Ming had told her about. After all, this was an entirely new part of herself. Or maybe it wasn't that new, after all. Maybe it had been there all along, just waiting for the right moment—or the right dream, maybe—to free it. Well, she was glad this part of her was finally free.

Isa paid her fare and got on the bus, settling into an empty seat next to a man reading a trashy-looking book. He glanced up at her when she sat down, almost as if he was assessing her for date-ability. Or fuck-ability, most likely. But maybe she was putting off a different sort of vibe, now that she'd gone all girl-crazy, as he didn't seem to assess her for long before he stopped looking at her and went back to his book. Maybe this "I only like women now" energy she might now be putting off would limit the day-to-day annoyances of men hitting on her.

But upon getting off the bus, she watched as three construction workers exited a restaurant. And they were watching, too, as one whistled and the other one said something so crude Isa thought he should have been punched in the balls. *Oh well, can't have it all.* Instead of going over to him and slamming her fist into his crotch, she yelled something about what he liked to do with his mother, and he and his buddies cracked up.

The world could do with a few less men like that, Isa thought, and a few more like…well, she hadn't really had any good examples of what good men were like in her life, so she decided to just go with Gandhi and Jesus. That would have to do for now.

Back inside her place, she chugged some OJ out of the carton, then walked over to the couch. Even though she'd slept well the night before, she was incredibly tired. Maybe it was the sex, maybe it was the confusion. Whatever it was, she couldn't stay awake very much longer. But then a thought occurred to her—did her sudden tiredness have anything to do with Lilith?

And here she was, Isa thought as she shut her eyes, doing something she'd never done before—juggling two potential partners. It seemed, in a word, tacky. And unfortunate, for both of them. Not that Ming could ever know about Lilith. Ming would think she was crazy as a—but the first seconds of a delicious, deep sleep interrupted that thought.

❖

Isa was walking into an amusement park, full of women—not a single man to be seen. Not that there's anything wrong with that, Isa thought. And then a hand on her shoulder caused her to jump a little, but when she turned, she was delighted to see Lilith.

"Hey! I guess I get to be with you today. That's great." Isa grinned at her, a grin she hoped Lilith saw as believable, because you might say Lilith had first dibs on her, and now here Isa was, sleeping with someone else.

"Yes, but she's in the real world, and I'm only in your dreams." Right. Lilith could read her mind in the dreams Isa had of her. Or she could at least some of the time, it seemed. Well, there went any chance of holding back information.

"I saw you with her, you know," Lilith said, taking Isa's hand in hers, very gently, and bringing it to her mouth, giving it a light kiss—almost just a brush of her lips across it, more than a kiss, but it still stirred Isa's libido into full alert.

"We can't…I mean, there are people around here," Isa said, and Lilith nodded, as if to agree.

"Yes, I saw you with her, and while I didn't watch while you had sex—I felt that would have been rude—I did see you on your date. Just bits of it…the lunch, eating dinner together. I know you can't have any of that with me, at least in your real life," and Lilith sighed, softly, averting her eyes, "but I hope I can still give you some nice times, even outside of the bedroom. Although I have far less practice with such interactions. None, to be honest, at least in the dream world."

"Actually, I love amusement parks," Isa told her, and squeezed her hand, hoping that would reassure Lilith, hoping that her next words would help reassure her, too. "Especially the food. And the roller coasters, as long as I have someone's ear to scream into."

"What would you like to do first, darling?" Isa had noticed Lilith's eyes light up as she'd complimented her choice of location. Good. Isa wanted this to be as fun for Lilith as it was for her. "I must admit, I don't have much experience with parks like this, as I've just read about them in books. I hope I got everything right."

"As long as everything is up to the highest standards of safety, we'll be fine. I'm sure you did great." Isa gestured toward all the rides and stands in front of them. "It looks perfect, just like in real life."

"That's wonderful, then. All right, where should we begin?"

Enjoying the feel of Lilith's soft, warm hand in hers, Isa pulled her toward the first fun-looking ride in front of them. It was a smallish, bright-green roller coaster, the kind where people hung upside down for bits of the ride. Isa figured since this was a dream that it would be perfectly safe, although in real life she didn't care how safe the ride's controller said it was; she did *not* want to be turned upside down or have her legs dangling hundreds of feet above the ground. But this was a chance to try out one of the scariest rides, without any worries. And with an absolutely beautiful woman beside her, as well.

"This looks...interesting," Lilith said, eyeing the roller coaster warily. "Will it...I mean, I made everything in here completely safe...but will it be...scary?" She looked at Isa, her eyes wide open. It was quite obvious to Isa that she was incredibly nervous.

"You'll be fine," Isa told her, wrapping Lilith in a quick hug—a hug that wound up making Isa wish they were alone, because between the clove and cinnamon scent of Lilith's hair and the feel of her flesh and tits pressed up against Isa, it took all she had to not suggest they fuck right there. But Isa realized she wanted to enjoy this date with Lilith. Maybe this wasn't all about sex, after all. It didn't seem to be for Lilith...and Isa was starting to think it wasn't just Lilith's body, or her touch, that kept Lilith on her mind.

But now it was time to ride the coaster. The woman who ran the ride buckled them into their seats, but the part that went through Isa's legs felt a little strange. Almost like it was vibrating. Isa glanced at Lilith—she was grinning. "I thought I'd make one small adjustment on this ride…seemed like with it being as terrifying as it looks to be, at least you and I can get a few orgasms out of it."

"*Now* you're thinking, cutie!" Isa grabbed Lilith's hand as the ride started up, and as they climbed up the first steep hill, her pleasure climbed along with them and her lower body got warm as the safety strap buzzed away on her clit. And so, instead of screaming from fear as the coaster raced down the first dip, she screamed with pleasure, feeling herself falling and coming all at once. What a smart woman that Lilith was!

Isa glanced at Lilith out of the corner of her eye and Lilith was looking like she was either close to coming or already headed toward her second orgasm. And then, as they were quickly flipped upside down, Lilith squeezed Isa's hand tight, tighter, and Isa heard Lilith's own cries, right near her ear, which sent her over the edge again, her second orgasm of the ride.

And there were a few more where those came from, to the point where Lilith and Isa had to lean on each other for support as they got off the ride, both of them grinning and laughing.

"You ladies have fun?" the amusement-park worker asked them, a slightly confused look on her face.

"Oh, yeah!" Isa said, laughing again. "Best time I've ever had on one of those."

They both—slowly—regained their ability to stand upright, but Lilith kept her arm around Isa's waist, and so Isa did the same to her. She felt so nice, Isa thought, and then another thought followed. Isa could just enjoy the feel of Lilith's side touching hers and have it not be sexual, just pleasant, almost comforting.

"Now, what kind of food do you want to start with? I should have you know, you can eat as much as you want here and not gain a pound."

Isa laughed. Well, that made this dream even better. "How about we start with some corn dogs and curly fries, then maybe a funnel cake and a cinnamon bun."

"I don't know what those things are, but considering your refined taste in women—myself, for example—I guess that they're delicious. Just like you," and she pecked Isa on the cheek.

"Thanks! And yes, they're all really good, especially the funnel cakes. Not everyday food, but good on occasion. Some things should only be that way—just an occasional indulgence."

After Isa said that, it looked like Lilith became lost in thought. What was it that she'd said?

Lilith's concentration on the here and now came back moments later, and she looked at Isa and smiled, although her smile looked a little empty, like there wasn't as much joy in it as there had been before. "So, is it...corn dogs first?"

They went to a stand selling corn dogs and curly fries, and they each got their own—completely free, of course, since it was a dream—and settled down onto a bright-pink bench. "You don't see too many benches this color," Isa said around her first bite of corn dog.

But instead of responding to her, Lilith moaned. "Oh my, is that *ever* delicious. Where do you humans come up with such genius ideas? The person who invented these deserves an award."

"And just wait until you try the curly fries," Isa said to her, nudging Lilith's side with a chuckle.

Bites of those brought more moans from Lilith, and when Isa told her to add ketchup, well, she hadn't seen Lilith that happy since her last orgasm. They made record time in finishing the food, doing their best to talk with their mouths full of corn dog and fries.

Isa learned that Lilith lived in a world where all human dreams came from. She was, of course, one of the Dreammakers in charge of sexual dreams, but she told Isa that there were other factions, too. Isa felt grateful that she hadn't befriended one of the nightmare Dreammakers instead, but perhaps if she had, they could have helped with her horrible nightmares.

Lilith asked Isa about the terrible dreams she sometimes had—reading her mind yet again—but Isa told her she didn't want to talk about them, and emptied her mind of them as best she could. After all, Isa wanted to have a nice time with her, and her nightmare creature wasn't welcome here, not in this place of joy and pleasure and good company.

They ended the date with a ride on the Ferris wheel, watching as the sun fell lower and lower, the sky in front of them a wash of lush purples and glowing shades of pink. Isa held Lilith's hand, smiling the entire time.

"I had a great time, you know," Isa told her as they were once again swept up into the air.

"I did as well." Lilith let go of Isa's hand and put her arm around Isa, holding her tight, holding Isa like she never wanted to let go.

❖

Isa woke up from the dream with a smile on her face. It had been lovely, the time she'd spent with Lilith, and she wasn't surprised in the least when she saw a small bag of cotton candy, rainbow-colored, sitting on the floor next to her couch.

She was definitely juggling two women now, and she had to admit—Lilith might actually be winning, despite the fact that she lived entirely in the land of dreams. Isa might never walk on a beach with her, or make love to Lilith in her bed, or eat takeout and watch a corny movie with her…at least, not outside of her dreams. In them, though, all that—and much, much more—was possible. But did Isa really want to give up on having a woman in her reality, on having a woman outside of her dreams? She didn't really know—she really couldn't answer that question. At least, not yet.

❖

Shae paced back and forth in her bedroom. Sleeping had become almost impossible, worries cropping up in her head over the past few nights. Would all go according to plan? Would she succeed? She had to succeed, because an amazing amount rode on whether things would work out in her favor.

She'd told the rest of her Nightmaremakers to leave her be for the time being, that she was caring for Amaya, who happened to be exhausted from her travels. What she hadn't told them was that she'd shut down all communication between their village and Amaya's, using all the power she could pull from Amaya. After all, she had to shield her village's Nightmaremakers from finding out they were cut off. In all the years she'd reigned as her village's leader, they'd never realized her true personality, one that hungered for power. No, she had kept it completely hidden. Hidden behind fake smiles and kind words. Hidden behind fake loyalty toward that damned queen of theirs. Rebecca, who had power that rightfully should have been *hers*, damn it all!

But now she was getting ready to come out of hiding; she was ready to show everyone the true Shae. She had already begun to steal Amaya's power, and the strength and magic Shae had gained from her was now begging for release. And she had the perfect plan, a plan to steal even more power.

Yes, she realized, her lips curling up into a dark smile, yes, this would all work perfectly.

Now, though, it was time to check on Amaya and make sure she was still deeply asleep, dreaming of all the horrors Shae had placed in the sexual Dreammaker's head. Horrors that would all turn into realities, soon enough.

CHAPTER EIGHTEEN

L ilith stepped out of the mirror in a delightful mood. She might not have swayed Isa entirely to her side (and away from that annoying Ming woman), but she still had time to win her over completely. If only she could enter Isa's reality. She would even give up her powers, even give up the dream world, for just one night in Isa's arms, in Isa's bed. In Isa's world. But no, she wasn't in love with her. No, she was just very fond of her, and liked her more than the other humans she'd interacted with. That was *all*.

She went through the rest of her day in a dreamy haze. Her friends commented on it at dinner, and she just told them that she'd given someone an especially hot dream. And yes, her dream with Isa *had* been hot, but that wasn't all…it had been lovely, too, and romantic, and…and *nothing*. Dreammakers weren't supposed to get involved with humans, not at all…not like this. So she would have to keep it simple and light with Isa from now on. Perhaps just sex dreams for the rest of their time together. If she could manage that…

Even in her haze, though, she had started wondering when Amaya would get back. What was taking her so long? And who was this mysterious creature controlling the humans' dreams, attacking them while they were supposed to be sleeping peacefully?

But that night, they'd still had no word from Amaya, and people all around the village were starting to worry, Lilith included. After all, Isa wasn't the only important thing right at the moment, she had to remind herself. People were getting hurt in their city, and something had to be done about it.

And then the meeting hall's bell sounded, shortly after dinner; all the Dreammakers who were free then gathered in the hall.

Francisco—Amaya's place-keeper, as Lilith thought of him—stood on the stage, pacing back and forth. He looked very worried, and that concern spread through the hall, catching the Dreammakers' attention, causing them to talk nervously among themselves.

"Let's get started," he called out, and he stopped pacing. "I have some horrible news. Amaya is missing, and we have lost our ability to travel to the Nightmaremakers' land."

A slight bit of panic broke out in the hall. Men and women turned to each other, and tense murmurs traveled throughout the crowd.

"Silence!" At this command, the talking died down.

"We think it has to do with the mysterious creature who is affecting people's dreams," Francisco said. "We think it is to blame. So I want all of you to watch out for any signs of it—of this evil creature—and you should be as careful as you possibly can. If you see anything out of the ordinary, exit the dream as fast as possible and report back to me. That is all."

As the Dreammakers shuffled out of the hall, everyone was talking; everyone was clearly shaken up. Some were just a little scared, some much more than a little. Lilith's closest friend, Aileen, caught up to her a few minutes later, as Lilith, her head buzzing with worried thoughts, walked toward home.

"Hello, dear," Aileen said, hooking her arm through Lilith's. "Have any thoughts on the matter?"

"I…don't know. Not really. Not yet. It sounds like something horrible has happened to Amaya, but I don't want to think that, not at all, even though it's quite possibly true."

They were a good distance away from everyone else by now, and Lilith thought, just for a moment, of telling her friend about Isa. But as close as they were, it wasn't a good idea, she decided. No, she would not be telling Aileen about the lovely human. Not yet, at least.

"What do you think, Aileen?" she asked instead.

"Well, someone needs to figure out what's going on. And fast! Who knows what kind of havoc this creature can wreak. Who knows how much it can ruin. It also sounds almost as if its power is growing."

"Perhaps it is. Do you have any idea how to find it? I almost feel the need to go after it myself," Lilith said in a hushed tone. People were still nearby, after all.

"Oh no, no, dear, *no*. That's a horrible idea! I know that we are in jeopardy, that we are threatened, and so are the humans that we help to have sweet, sexy dreams, but you should *not* go after it, not on your own. And I cannot help you, either, as you well know."

"Yes, of course. I'm sorry, I just got…excited, I suppose."

They were now at Lilith's house, and so Aileen kissed her good-bye and headed off toward her own home. Lilith's friend didn't have the power to enter into dreams any more. That was why Aileen couldn't help her. But should Lilith take her advice and not try to solve this all herself? If she tried, she could possibly get hurt—or worse. But if she didn't…was there a risk for Isa? Could Isa get hurt? Could Isa get *killed*? Maybe that was rather unlikely, but more than that, it was completely unacceptable. She would just have to watch over Isa a little more carefully.

Lilith got out her bowl, filled it with water, and put in the necessary herbs and leaves. She might not get as much sleep as usual now, or have as much freedom, but what did sleep—or even freedom—matter when you were helping someone dear to you stay alive?

When she looked into the bowl, she saw that Isa was picking up her phone. Was it Ming who was calling her? She certainly hoped not. And no, it turned out to be another woman. An older one. Lilith watched raptly, wondering now who this woman was and what Isa intended to do with her. Then Isa asked the woman a very surprising question, and the woman began to speak of her dreams, and Lilith became far more interested.

CHAPTER NINETEEN

After her nap, and her lovely dream, Isa put the cotton candy in the kitchen, even though she wanted to eat it right then and see how food from the dream world measured up against human food—although perhaps it *was* human food? She couldn't really know for sure until she tasted it. But she needed to eat something a little healthier than that for dinner, especially since, thanks to Lilith, she'd slept right through lunch. So she put together a salad and heated some canned potato-leek soup. It wasn't as good as the meal the night before, and it wouldn't be preceded by really hot sex, either. At least, not in *my* reality, Isa thought.

After dinner, she settled in front of the TV to watch an old movie she owned—one of the 1940s Sherlock Holmes films, with the incredibly handsome Basil Rathbone starring in it. But this time around, he wasn't doing much for her. No, instead she kept noticing the gorgeous woman with the dark hair and intense, beautiful eyes.

And then, around nine o'clock, her phone rang.

"Hello?"

"Hi...Isa?" The person's voice sounded familiar, but Isa couldn't quite place it. Not yet, at least.

"Yep, it's me."

"It's Iriana."

"Oh, hi! How are you?" What a pleasant surprise!

"Just fine. You wanted to get together again, was that right?"

"Yeah, I did," Isa said. And then she decided to take the plunge. "Actually, I wanted to talk to you about something in particular, something we have in common."

"Oh, have you taken up a paintbrush, my dear?"

"No. It's about your dreams."

Iriana gasped, and then they both were silent for a few minutes. Isa spoke again. "I don't mean to bother you, I really don't, and I know this may sound crazy, but…did you ever think that woman was real?"

"Real?" Iriana sounded shocked, but was it because of Isa's crazy question, or because Iriana actually believed her dream woman existed? "I…well…maybe…maybe we should meet up tomorrow and talk about this. In person. At my studio. Would that work for you? I mean, are you free?"

"Yes, I am. What time?"

"Oh, how about ten? If you like pastries, good ones, I can get us some wonderful croissants from the place down the block from me. And coffee…do you drink coffee?" Iriana's voice was shaking a little. Had Isa struck a nerve with her words? Maybe she had. *Hopefully* she had.

"Yep, usually mochas."

"Then that's what I'll get us. See you at ten. Good-bye." And before waiting for Isa's own "good-bye," she hung up.

Isa could hardly wait until morning to find out the truth about Iriana and her dream woman. But sadly, before morning came, she had a very intense dream. It wasn't one that contained Lilith. No, instead of sweet dreams of her own dream woman, Isa had another horrible nightmare.

❖

Again, she was being chased. Chased by her nightmare man. And this time, they were running through a hallway, and Isa saw a woman with an axe, hacking away at a door. It was a very long hallway, and Isa was far ahead of the silver-toothed monster of a man, but he was gaining on her, like he always did, yelling what he always yelled. "Help me get free! Free me!"

As she came up to the woman with the axe, Isa grabbed her and pulled her back from the door.

"But I have to kill her," the woman whined, her voice pitiful and strained. "I'm supposed to…you've got to let me!"

"No, no, you mustn't. This is just a dream, and you need to wake up."

And how did Isa know that? Was it just a dream, like she'd said? Did that mean all of this—everything around her—wasn't real?

❖

And then Isa woke up, drenched with sweat, and she felt, down to her very bones, that the dream had been as real as the bed she lay on, as the room around her, as the droplets of sweat on her skin.

It was about five a.m., and she couldn't stop shaking, so she went into the bathroom and took as hot a shower as she could handle. After she had dried off, she went into the living room and read one of her most comforting books, *The Hobbit.* But it didn't soothe her as much as usual, and she was almost entirely unable to get lost in it, still having an impossible time shaking her fear from the dream, her fear of that horrible man, and the horrible things that he seemed to cause.

A bit after eight, as she finished some oatmeal she'd intended to be comfort food, a strange thought crossed her mind. She opened her laptop and went online, to check the morning news. It took some searching, but there it was. A woman had been arrested in a hotel downtown, after hacking down one of the doors with an axe. Isa swore, the shock from what she read running across her skin like pinpricks. This could *not* be real.

But there were her dreams with Lilith, and so perhaps... perhaps there were other things, other dreams, which were real as well. She shivered at the thought, cold despite the heat flowing through the vents near her couch.

What did this mean, though? And why her? Why was *she* the one having these horrible dreams? And had she saved someone's life in her dream? Furthermore, had the previous nightmares been real, too? After thinking for a few moments, she decided to look back to the dates of her last nightmares and only a short while later, she came across a report of a house fire. Luckily, the man inside had survived the fire, only needing to spend one night in the hospital.

So...Isa was—perhaps—the cause of these two events, but was she the savior in each event as well? All of it was something to ask Lilith about, she decided. She would have to ask her in their next dream together, because maybe Lilith knew something about this. Maybe she could even stop Isa's nightmare creature from striking again.

But by the time Isa reached that thought, it was nine fifteen, and it would take the rest of the time between now and ten to get to Iriana's. So she threw together an outfit and rushed downstairs to the bus. Maybe some answers would come from this visit, answers about dream women. She didn't think Iriana would have any idea about her nightmare man, though, so she decided to keep that part to herself. No reason to scare the poor woman, after all.

Isa spent the whole ride to Iriana's place thinking about her latest nightmare, as well as the news report. And then she started to think about all the dreams she'd ever had about this creature.

One strange thing was that, up until now, no one else had been in them, just that horrific creature chasing her, yelling that he wanted her to free him. And up until now, she hadn't thought much of the dreams, just that they were terrifying and she wanted them to go away, forever. But now that people were potentially getting hurt because of them—and now that Isa was, just maybe, stopping worse things from happening—she wondered about what the nightmare creature meant when he told her to "free" him. And why did she have this power in the dreams, the power to save the people in them? Or was she imagining her involvement? Were these real-life events not connected to her dreams at all? Either could be true, she decided, which troubled her deeply.

She arrived at Iriana's a little after ten, and Iriana let her right in after only one knock. Today, the woman looked a little disheveled and had faint bags under her eyes. Maybe she'd had a bad night too, Isa thought, although she doubted they'd dreamt of the same thing. At least, she sincerely hoped not.

"Have a seat," Iriana said, gesturing toward the couch. "I'll bring the coffee and croissants." Isa sat down, and Iriana carried the food and coffee on the same tray as during Isa's last visit over here. This time it held a jar of raspberry jam, the croissants, and two to-go cups with what smelled like mochas.

"Thanks for having me over." Isa took a sip of her mocha as Iriana sat down next to her.

They ate and drank in silence for a few moments.

"So…" Isa said. Then she fell silent—after all, where did you begin with something like this?

"Yes." Iriana glanced at Isa, then turned her eyes to the tray. A moment later, she cleared everything off it, placing the food and coffee to either side of the tray. Isa looked down at it again, seeing the sleeping woman on it. But this time she saw the woman more clearly, saw that she looked just like Iriana, minus a few wrinkles and a few more years.

"You see this tray? This beautiful tray? This will sound crazy, but the woman in those paintings gave it to me. My dream woman. My angel. She started coming to me in my dreams in my early twenties, just…sex dreams at first. Frivolous. The dreams were full of pleasure—but nothing more. After a while…after a while we began to talk instead of screw, or at least, to talk *before* we screwed. And she amazed me, this dream woman. Every time I dreamt of her, I would wake up with a smile. And then… then she told me she actually existed one night, and I woke up to this tray in the morning. A gift from her. I wanted to return the favor, so I started painting her, sculpting her, making her into art, because she was as beautiful as can be.

"But then, about ten years ago, the dreams just stopped. No explanation, they just went away. And I haven't had a single dream of her ever since. Sex dreams, yes, but not her, not my girl, not any more. I have no idea *why* she's gone, or *where* she's gone, just that she is—gone. And I will probably never see her again. And I know this all must sound crazy," and here Iriana looked up at Isa, and Isa saw that she was crying. "I know it must, but you made it sound as if…as if maybe you were dreaming of a woman, too."

"Yes, I am. Her name is Lilith, and she's beautiful, too, and generous…and really great in bed," Isa added, feeling a little embarrassed to say that to someone she hardly knew.

But Iriana laughed at that final part of the sentence. "Yes, that's always a bonus in a partner. But…what about Ming? I wasn't dating anyone while I was still dreaming of my woman. So I didn't have…I mean, are you confused? About the two of them? About whether Lilith is even real, like I was with my own dream woman? I must admit that it's a relief to finally know I wasn't crazy, after all these years of wondering." One side of Iriana's mouth was turned up a little now, and she wasn't crying any more. "God, it's such a relief to know. If only I could have the relief of seeing her again as well. Just once. Just…once."

And then Iriana began to sob, and even though they had only just met the day before, Isa knew it would be okay to take Iriana in her arms and hold her as she cried. She shook with each sob, her whole body showing so clearly how much this woman had meant to her.

But if Isa's Lilith were taken away, too? Just like that? Gone forever, no more visits, no more dreams, not even an explanation why? Isa realized then that losing Lilith would definitely make her sad. Maybe not *this* sad, not filled to the brim with pain like Iriana, but yes, it would be a loss. How much of a loss, though? Isa was unable to figure out the answer to that question just yet. And then there was Ming. Though…maybe things were moving too fast with her, Isa thought…and maybe they were moving too slowly with Lilith. Was that really how Isa felt? But this woman—Lilith—she…she was *real*. Isa knew that much for sure now, thanks to Iriana.

This jumble of thoughts tumbled around in Isa's head as she held Iriana, as Iriana cried. She had to have years of pain within her, Isa thought, held back because she couldn't tell anyone what she knew to be true—that the woman whom she had loved, and seemed to still love, was just as real as Isa was. After all, who would believe something like that? Isa certainly did, but it had been Iriana's secret and hers alone, for years. Too many of them. And now it was out, and Isa wondered if now, maybe Iriana was a little freer from the pain—because it was known, at least to Isa. And because Iriana now knew that she hadn't been wrong, that her dream woman had really existed.

After what seemed like quite a while, but could easily have just been mere minutes, Iriana made an effort to pull herself together. She got up and tore a few paper towels from a roll by the kitchen sink, blowing her nose with a loud *honk* after drying her eyes. Iriana walked back over to Isa and sat down. "Now," she said, a weak smile on her face, "why don't we try to enjoy breakfast. Which is now more of a lunch than a breakfast, thanks to me."

"Don't worry about it, really," Isa told her, patting her on the knee. "I can only imagine how hard all of this has been for you, to hold all that in for years, that secret. I just hope…I hope that me knowing now helps."

"Oh, my, does it ever! It's like…it's like a dam breaking, you know, but one made up of pain, and lies, a dam that held the truth at bay…one which stopped me from moving on. I know now—she's never coming back to me. Time to move on to the next part of my life, time to find a new muse."

But maybe she's not gone for good, Isa thought. Maybe there's some way to reconnect you and your girl.

They finished the food slowly, and Isa told Iriana more about Lilith—leaving certain details to Iriana's imagination, of course. And while Isa talked about Lilith, she tried to decide—Lilith or Ming? Which reality did she want to commit to? Then and there, she decided to go on another date with Ming. She had to figure out how she really felt about her. And hopefully, Lilith would reappear soon, in another dream, and Isa could use it to help decide about Lilith as well. Both her last date with Ming and her last "date" with Lilith had been nice—lovely, even. But which had been better? That had to be decided soon—because, after all, Isa couldn't string both of them along forever.

CHAPTER TWENTY

The next day, Isa called Ming, and they set up a date. But first, she needed to do some writing. Even though her life was pretty much chaos at the moment, she couldn't stop writing. She still had to eat, after all. And pay rent. And buy potential girlfriends flowers, perhaps.

The flowers Lilith had given her, though, had started to wilt by then, and some of the petals were turning brown. Their glow had also dimmed greatly. Maybe, Isa thought, that was because they didn't belong in her world, a world devoid of magic and people who could bring humans dreams. She couldn't quite talk herself into throwing the flowers away, not just yet, but at the risk that Ming might spot them, should she come into Isa's bedroom this night, Isa decided to hide them in her closet, with hopes that the slight glow from the door's crack wouldn't be noticeable.

After Isa had called Ming, she'd called Martin, and he had come and picked up as much of his stuff as he could. His friend Barry brought some help in the form of a bright-orange VW bus, and Isa even helped Martin carry out some bags and boxes of his things. The apartment seemed a little emptier by the time he'd left, but it seemed much more comfortable—like it was hers now, entirely hers. She might share it again at some point, but certainly not with a man. Yes, never again.

She got as much writing done as she could, then hopped on the bus, to meet Ming downtown for dinner and a movie. Dinner wound up being at a tapas restaurant in the trendiest part of town, and it was certainly not cheap, but Isa did manage to talk Ming into going Dutch. It was really a challenge convincing her, though. Chivalry wasn't dead after all…at least when a woman was your date, apparently. But Isa certainly didn't mind said chivalry. It was nice—very nice—that Ming wanted to be so romantic.

Then they went to a rather depressing romantic drama. Part of why it was depressing was because Isa was just starting to notice how invisible gay women were in pop culture. Of course, they weren't invisible if the women were hot, but then they were only visible because of straight men, it seemed. Most of Isa's boyfriends had been big fans of lesbian porn, at least the ones who hadn't been smart enough to hide their porn collections from her prying eyes. But, she now realized, it wasn't "lesbian" at all. That wasn't what it was really like to sleep with a woman, all those fake moans and the deep-throating of dildos, not to mention the tongues that didn't look like they knew what to do, not even slightly. No, all subterfuge, all fake, all gloss and veneer. Real sex with a real lesbian, oh, that was so much better than those falsified male-fantasy versions captured on film. Isa smiled at her discovery, at the lovely thoughts of what *real* lesbian sex was like. Oh, yeah, it was so much better when the woman actually wanted to be touching her partner…*way* better.

And then, after dinner and the movie, Isa proceeded to prove to herself, yet again, how much better real lesbian sex was than she had previously thought it could be. She and Ming had exceptionally hot sex back at Ming's place, but Isa couldn't talk herself into spending the night. She really felt rude begging off sleeping over, and Ming looked a little hurt, but Isa just lied and told her she hadn't been sleeping well, and that she really needed her own bed that night. Which was only slightly untrue. The nightmares had been messing with her sleep a fair amount, actually. But that ignored the fact that she'd slept just fine in Ming's bed a few nights back.

Isa was incredibly confused, feeling pulled between these two women. Which one of them was the right one to choose? She still couldn't say, and so she tried to just shut it out of her mind on the bus ride home, but wound up failing miserably.

Once at home, she made herself some chamomile tea, in hopes it would calm her frayed nerves, nerves that seemed to be at high alert these past few days. Between learning about Dreammakers, having her partially real nightmares, and juggling two women, she had far too much going on, both in her life and in her head. And in her dreams, too.

Would she dream about Lilith tonight? She hoped she would. But did that answer her question? Did the fact that she hadn't spent the night with Ming, and that she was hoping to dream about Lilith, well, did that mean she had made her choice? Oh, fucking hell, who knew? *She* certainly didn't.

Isa had one more cup of tea and just barely managed to relax enough to go to sleep, but only after about an hour of tossing and turning, about an hour of "Lilith or Ming?" "Lilith or Ming?" "Ming or Lilith?" again and again, and these thoughts drowned out anything else she could have been thinking of.

Before she had gotten into bed, though, Isa had taken her dream-flowers out of the closet. They still glowed just the tiniest bit, and they still smelled of jasmine, although it was fainter now, so subtle she had to bury her nose in them to catch the scent. Would her dreams tonight help with making her choice? Would Lilith even show up in them? Isa hoped having the flowers by her bedside would somehow draw Lilith to her, that they would somehow invite Lilith into her dreams. And, maybe, just maybe, they did.

❖

Here Isa was, back at the mansion once more, and this time she knew what she wanted, at least in this dream—Lilith. Lilith, and no one else. No gorgeous men, no orgies, no Ming. She now had plenty of Ming in the real world, after all. No, here Isa wanted one person and one person alone—a woman with garnet-red hair and rich, gold-colored eyes.

And Lilith seemed to read Isa's mind (or, possibly, she actually had). Because lying out on a silk-covered mattress, surrounded by softly glowing candles and plates of food, was Lilith. She was draped with a black silk sheet, contrasting in the loveliest way with her pale, beautiful skin, and she looked so very happy to see Isa, with a smile appearing on her face the very second Isa came into view.

"Hello, darling! It's so good to see you again. I hope you're as happy to see me as I am to see you." Lilith was grinning, her whole face lit up, and her eyes, with their golden glow maybe a little brighter than usual, were crinkled up just the slightest, loveliest amount in the far corners.

"I definitely am," Isa said. Yes, she was very glad to see Lilith, she now knew. Happier about seeing her here than she would have expected, in fact. So—this was the time to decide how strongly she felt about Lilith. To decide if she preferred her to Ming. And she realized the answer to that question just a few moments later.

She walked over to Lilith, but instead of doing something seductive, or something sexual, Lilith rose from the bed and enveloped Isa in her arms. Yes, Lilith was naked, but this wasn't just a passionate hug. It was a *heartfelt* one. One that told Isa how she felt about Lilith. And…well, there wasn't even close to a strong-enough word, but as Isa let her feelings, her emotions toward this woman, ripple through her, they pierced right into

Isa's heart. Was this...love? One look at Lilith's face told Isa it was, and a few seconds more of staring into Lilith's eyes made it seem as if Lilith felt the same way, or possibly, she might have felt even more. But it only seemed that way for a second, because Lilith's smile disappeared only a little bit later.

"Why don't you sit with me, enjoy some of the food I've set out for us," Lilith said, sitting down on the bed, and she reclined in such a perfect way that it had to be intentional. She seemed to know exactly how well her body's position showed off her perfection. Not that Isa didn't appreciate her perfection, but it seemed to her like Lilith had put on a mask, a disguise of sorts.

Maybe she didn't want Isa to know how she felt about her. And maybe, Isa thought, she should hide how she felt about Lilith, too. Because Isa was in no way certain that Lilith felt love toward her the way Isa felt it toward Lilith. Or if Lilith did feel the same amount of love, she didn't seem to feel comfortable with how she felt. Isa didn't know why this might be, but she decided she had to keep her own feelings hidden, too. She didn't want to risk letting Lilith know, not yet, not when Lilith hadn't made her own feelings clear yet. But would Lilith just pull Isa's thoughts right out of her head, like she seemed to almost always do? Couldn't Lilith just read her mind and see how Isa felt?

But it seemed Lilith wasn't dipping into Isa's thoughts at the moment, so instead of professing her undying love, Isa sat down next to her, legs crossed. Lilith waved her hand, and suddenly Isa was as naked as she was. And Isa didn't mind, not in the least.

She started to reach out toward some grapes, but Lilith's hand was faster. She brushed past Isa's hand and grabbed one, placing it between her own lips. Then she leaned toward Isa, bringing her lips so very close to Isa's, and slowly slid the grape in between

Isa's lips, her tongue teasing the opening of Isa's mouth. "Let's forget about the food, my darling," Lilith murmured, her lips so close, so tantalizingly close. And then she closed the minute distance between her lips and Isa's, and her kiss was filled with passion, with an intensity Isa hadn't felt with her yet.

Lilith tackled Isa to the mattress and, suddenly, cuffs appeared around Isa's wrists. She had never been restrained before, but she knew instantly that it was something she loved, something that did a hell of a lot for her. It also did a lot to her cunt, so very wet now, and just in mere seconds. Then Lilith slid Isa's thighs apart, diving right into her cunt, causing Isa to squirm, to fight the restraints, causing her to buck against Lilith's lips. She had Isa coming in mere moments, with a tongue that Isa had to admit was far more skilled than Ming's. Which probably meant Lilith had had more practice. That thought came with a slight bit of pain, but she pushed it all away, because it was her that Lilith was here with right now, not anyone else. It was her, time and time again, whom Lilith had chosen to come to, to get off, to go on dates with, and kiss and screw and talk to. It was Isa she seemed to want to be with. At least right now.

Lilith's tongue got Isa off only a little bit later, and then again, and then Isa lost count of the orgasms, each one better than the last, until the restraints disappeared. And then Isa pulled Lilith up, on top of her, and kissed Lilith's lips—long, deep, rough—and flipped her over, and now the restraints were on *Lilith's* wrists, and now Isa's mouth was shoved up against *her* cunt. Isa licked her, tasted her, sucking her labia into her mouth, then went straight for Lilith's clit, wanting to give Lilith as much pleasure as she possibly could. And soon, Lilith was the one who was crying out in pleasure, and now she was the one who was coming, over and over again, bucking against Isa's mouth, fighting against the restraints. And fuck, but this went so far beyond Isa's experiences with Ming. Her body's response to

Lilith had made up her mind a little bit more. And so—as much as Isa had trouble admitting it—had her heart. But what about Lilith? Did she feel the same way?

There was, of course, the fact that there was no way for them to be together, Isa thought, as she rose and kissed Lilith, letting their tastes mix upon each of their tongues. How could she and Lilith be together, if they were only able to meet in dreams? Was there a way for them to be together in the flesh, even in Lilith's reality? Then, Please, Isa thought, please, please let there be a chance of it. And please, let her feel the same way about me. Now Isa had to fight not to cry, worrying about these two things the entire time she kissed Lilith, barely able to pay attention to Lilith's fingers as they slipped inside her, rubbing and thrusting against Isa's G-spot, until Isa came again, gushing all over Lilith.

Was there a way for them to be together? Isa kissed Lilith one last time, then pushed herself up, looking into Lilith's gold, glowing eyes, assessing them. Did Isa see only her own love reflected back in them? Or did she see love from Lilith, as well?

❖

And then Isa woke up, a large wet spot soaking the bed beneath her. She got up, slowly, savoring what she could of the dream, of Lilith's touch, and of the way Lilith had looked at her when she had first entered the room. There *had* to be some love in Lilith's heart, Isa thought, because no one looked at someone that way if she felt nothing but lust. Was that right? Isa hoped so. Oh, did she ever hope so.

But now she had to clean up. It was six a.m., a little early to start her day, but any day starting with multiple orgasms had a good beginning, she thought with a smile. And any day that started with time spent with someone you loved had a good beginning, too. Even if they didn't feel the same way, and Isa felt a small ache in her chest, felt as it began to grow into something worse. She got into the shower, rinsing the sticky flesh between her legs with the removable showerhead. And then Isa got herself off again, just one more time, thinking of Lilith, imagining—and wishing—it was Lilith's hand touching her, and not her own.

CHAPTER TWENTY-ONE

When Lilith had left Isa's dream and walked back through her mirror, she was filled with sadness. She'd avoided reading Isa's mind while she was in her dream, avoided it entirely. Because if she had come across any thoughts that told her Isa didn't feel the same way—which seemed so very likely— it would just break her heart. And while her heart had never been broken before, she knew, for certain, that it would hurt. She didn't want to risk that happening, as possible as it was...as likely as it was. How could Isa fall for someone she could be with only in her dreams? A person whom she couldn't touch, couldn't get up with in the morning, and someone whom she could never talk to after a hard day? Someone who was available to her only while she was asleep? No...who on earth would want that?

And then there was the fact that she was dating that "Ming" woman. It was certainly understandable that Isa would date humans, people who were in the real world. People who she could touch, and kiss, and cuddle up next to. It was nice that she was starting to date a woman, instead of another man, but Lilith wanted that woman to be *her*. However, Lilith couldn't pass into Isa's world. She could enter her dreams as often as she liked, she could use her very special skill to take things from her reality to Isa's, but she couldn't move herself across the boundary between their worlds.

Was this actually *real* love, though? Just from a few brief encounters in Isa's dreams? Lilith hated that idea, but it seemed like it had to be real, that it had to be love. Having watched over Isa a number of times, with a touch of magic and a water-filled bowl, Lilith had noticed other things about Isa, other things to like. And beyond those things was the fact that they were lovely together when they were naked, when their bodies and fingers and lips touched. But Lilith concluded that maybe she shouldn't go into Isa's dreams any more. Or, at least, not for a while. She had to let Isa live in her own reality.

That would be nearly impossible to follow through, though, to avoid going into Isa's dreams, even for a short period of time. Probably *completely* impossible. Yes, she couldn't keep herself away from Isa, and it seemed...yes, it seemed that for the moment, at least, Isa didn't mind her presence.

She would not watch Isa any more while she was awake. She didn't want to see when Isa kissed Ming, when she slept with her (perish the thought!). It would hurt, to see this...it would be far too painful. It was hard enough to come into Isa's dreams looking like someone else (like Ming, as that was who it had seemed Isa wanted), but at least it was still herself beneath the veneer of Ming's face and body.

Lilith decided to go to her friend Aileen's house. Perhaps... perhaps if she told Aileen about her problems, she could get some advice. Aileen was one of the village's older inhabitants, so maybe she would have some knowledge of such a thing happening—of a Dreammaker falling for a human. So Lilith left her own home and headed toward her friend's.

Aileen was out in her garden when Lilith arrived a short while later, on her knees in the middle of a row of dirt, which she seemed to be planting something in. She didn't notice Lilith's approach, and so she jumped a little when Lilith first spoke.

"Hello, Aileen."

"Oh! Lilith!" Aileen slowly got off her knees and brushed a few strands of her silver-streaked red hair out of her face, managing to add a few streaks of dirt to her right cheek.

"You're…here," Lilith said, and brushed the dirt off Aileen's cheek.

"Can't help but get a little dirty when you're up to your elbows *in* dirt. So nice to see you, dear," and she wrapped her arms around Lilith. Her hands were covered in dirt, too, and Lilith sighed as quietly as she could. She would have to wash this dress when she got home. Oh well, she usually got a little dirty when she came over here, either because Aileen was digging in the dirt or because she got Lilith to help her with some planting.

"Would you like to come in for some tea?" Aileen asked. "I promise I'll wash my hands before I get out the glasses. Iced tea, since it's a little warm out today."

"That sounds nice. I am a little thirsty, actually."

Aileen wrapped her arm around Lilith's shoulders and led her inside, through the open door of her cottage.

Her friend kept a more modest house than most of the sexual Dreammakers, the walls a pale blue instead of the richer tones most of the Dreammakers in their village favored. She had only one piece of art, a sketch of a nude woman who faced away from whoever had drawn her. The rest of her home was subtle as well—a simple, white kitchen table, a few appliances, and a bed in the corner, as it was a one-room house, which was also unlike most of the homes in their village. She had told Lilith when Lilith had asked about it that she preferred a simple existence; plenty of excitement had filled her past. But they had never talked about one thing, the fact that Aileen never entered people's dreams any more. Lilith had asked her about it once, and that was the one time Aileen had ever taken a harsh tone with her, telling Lilith firmly that it was none of her business.

Today, though, she was all smiles, pouring them two large glasses of iced tea, then slicing a lemon and dropping a fourth of it into each tall, dark-blue glass. "So," she said, sitting down across from Lilith, "what brings you here?"

Lilith was silent for a few moments. Even though Aileen was her closest friend, this was still a taboo subject, so she hesitated to come right out and say it. She decided to begin as subtly as she could. "Have you...have you ever heard of a Dreammaker falling in love with a human?"

Aileen looked off over Lilith's shoulder, her eyes unfocused, almost like she was in another time or place for just a few seconds. "Yes, I have heard of something like that happening before." She turned back to Lilith, and a shrewd expression appeared on her face. "Is there a reason you are asking me this, dear?"

"I...yes, there is, but you must not tell anyone else." The words were just fighting to escape from Lilith's mouth, but she had to wait until Aileen had agreed to her request.

"Of course, that will be no trouble at all, if you are about to tell me what I think you are."

"I think I have fallen for someone."

"Yes?"

"For a human. Her name is Isabelle, and she loves to read, like me, and she's beautiful, and kind, and a skilled lover, especially for someone who has never been with a woman before." Now the words were rushing out, and Lilith couldn't stop them. "In a very short time, I've grown feelings for her. Strong ones. Which seems unlikely. Impossible, in fact. And it's unacceptable!" She couldn't help it. She pounded her fist on the table like a child complaining about the unfairness of life, a child who was throwing a temper tantrum because of something she felt was unfair. But Lilith was a grown woman, and she should have realized by now that life was entirely unfair and that, very often, you couldn't have what you wanted.

"Before you continue," Aileen said, a faint smile playing across her lips, "tell me. Do you like my sketch? The one on the wall in front of you?"

"Yes...yes, I do, but what does that have to do with my problem?" Lilith was confused. Why was Aileen asking about her taste in art at a time like this?

"You don't understand. Of course you don't. That woman there, in the sketch, that's someone I used to know. I met her a fair number of years ago, when I was also a fair bit younger. We met in dreams, of course, because she was a human. At first, we just engaged in sexual dalliances, but then, she began to make art for me, showing it to me in the dreams I brought her before we made love. Yes, made love, because I fell for this young woman, fell for her just like we aren't permitted to.

"But she lived in the human world, not in ours, and so I couldn't possibly have her in real life. To kiss her actual lips, to hold her actual hand, no, I couldn't have any of that. We continued to meet in her dreams for a great many years, and I watched her from time to time, in a bowl of water, exactly the way we aren't supposed to. We also aren't supposed to get involved with humans, and so when the current king of all us Dreammakers learned of my indiscretion, I was stripped of my powers. Although, to be quite honest, I gave them up gladly. Because if I couldn't be with her in real life, it was far too painful to be with her only in her dreams. Now, my dear, about your problem. I would advise you to keep away from this woman's dreams, but I know you won't. So just keep your feelings as quiet as you can, because although Rebecca is a far more just queen than King Eric ever was a king, it's still just not done, a Dreammaker falling for a human."

The beginnings of tears filled Lilith's eyes, and then she began to cry, unable to hold them back. "It's just not fair! We shouldn't be kept from loving humans, if we so choose!"

"But you do not choose who you love, my dear," Aileen said, placing a gentle hand on Lilith's shoulder. "It's impossible, like fighting with the sea. The tide does what it will, and so does the heart, and neither can be defeated in battle. I wish...I wish we had some way, both of us, to be with our women...with the women of our dreams.

"If only...but treasure the time you have with this woman, with this Isabelle, and pray that you do not get caught. Because then you will experience my own pain, and you will know what it's like to be kept away, forever, from the person you love. I wouldn't...I would never wish this upon you...or anyone, not even the king who took my powers away. Stay careful, and perhaps you may keep spending time with her. But keep this a secret. You must tell no one else. Now...would you like something to eat? I find it helps to eat something sweet when your heart is hurting."

"Yes," Lilith said, smiling faintly through her tears. "I could do with something sweet. Something sweet, to get rid of this bitter feeling crawling across my skin. Something just as sweet as Isabelle."

CHAPTER TWENTY-TWO

I sa had made up her mind about Lilith, or at least it seemed as if she had…but had Lilith made up her mind as well? Isa hadn't felt that tickle in the last dream she'd brought her—the tickle that seemed to tell Isa that Lilith was inside her head, reading her mind. Or at least, that's what she'd thought the sensation came from. So maybe Lilith didn't know how Isa felt about her. That made Isa feel a little safer, but quite a bit sadder, too. It felt…lonely, perhaps, not knowing if Lilith felt the same way. Lonely, too, because she wasn't there with Isa… and couldn't ever be there, either. Would Isa be willing to settle for this, just dreams? Not that they could be a "just," not with the way they made her feel, with the pleasure they brought her, both physical, and emotional, filling her to the brim with sensations. Romantic ones…and sexual ones too, of course.

Decisions had to be made, though, and so Isa gave Ming a call once it was a reasonable hour to reach her, a little after five thirty in the evening.

Ming answered on the second ring. "Hello?"

"Hey, Ming, it's Isa."

"Oh, hi! How are you doing? It's nice to hear from you."

"I'm doing well enough." Which wasn't exactly true, but… "Any chance you'll be free tonight?"

"I will be. Why, did you want to get together?"

"Yeah. How about my place this time? Maybe we could order a pizza, watch a movie or something. I have HBO, and they're showing a documentary tonight on Harvey Milk."

"Well, that doesn't sound super-upbeat, but the pizza will help. It'll give us something to throw at the screen."

Isa laughed at that. "Yeah, considering what my friend Vivian has told me about him, I doubt it'll fill me with joy and happy thoughts about humanity."

"Probably not. Well, when should I come over?"

"Any time you want. When should I order the pizza?"

"Maybe in about thirty minutes. And get whatever you want on it. I'm not picky."

"Okay, see you soon. Bye."

"Bye!"

Hopefully one more date would help Isa make up her mind about Ming, and about Lilith, once and for all. Although a large part of Isa had already made up its mind, not all of her had—her passionate side, yes, but not her rational one. That part of her was having a very hard time being convinced. It hadn't really ever accepted that Lilith was real, although Isa still knew she was. The flowers and the book were proof of that. And speaking of the flowers…

Isa went into her room. They still sat on her bedside table, the vase as beautiful as ever, but the flowers were a pale brown and didn't seem to be glowing at all anymore. Normally, flowers this brown should get thrown out, but Isa just couldn't get herself to do that, so she placed them on her chest of drawers, hoping they'd be out of the way enough for Ming to not see them, should they go into Isa's bedroom.

A little over thirty minutes later—which Isa spent pacing and then tidying up whenever the pacing got old—she ordered the pizza. Half Hawaiian, half pepperoni. Hopefully Ming would like at least one of them. A knock on the door came only a few minutes later, and Isa let Ming in.

Ming looked especially nice, with a low-cut tank top showing off the tits Isa had been appreciating for quite a while. The ones with the nipples that she certainly didn't mind sucking on, and so she decided to suggest a good way to fill up the time until the pizza came.

Ming didn't seem to mind her suggestion in the least. Soon, they were stripping off their clothes. And then Isa's mouth somehow found its way to Ming's nipples. She took each of Ming's nipples into her mouth, rolling them around, enjoying the feel of each bud of flesh against her tongue.

But as more clothes came off, Isa realized she was really having trouble concentrating. And she wasn't thinking of Ming. It wouldn't have taken Isa three guesses to figure out who she *was* thinking of, either.

Lilith, Lilith, Lilith.

Isa couldn't do this to Ming, so she pulled back from her. "We…as much as I hate to interrupt this…we have to talk."

Ming looked surprised for a few seconds, and then she sighed. "You're right, we do. This—I mean, I have trouble keeping my hands off you, but I have something I need to say, too, and I shouldn't have started undressing you, or let you undress me."

"Yeah, probably not."

"Well, since you brought it up, you should go first."

"Maybe we should put our shirts back on before we get started."

Ming chuckled, her laugh low and a little bit masculine. "Yep. I don't think I'll be able to concentrate with you sitting there in that amazingly sexy bra."

So they both put their shirts back on and sat down on Isa's couch. "I've…I've really enjoyed our time together, but I've been dating someone else while I've been dating you, and I've learned that…well, I hope this doesn't sound harsh, but I've learned that my feelings for her are incredibly strong." Here Isa was, admitting something out loud that she had barely admitted in her head. Yes, it was true, it was out. She loved Lilith.

"And before you go any further, I should say that the same is true for me. I wanted one last date with you to be sure of my choice…and entirely thanks to you, I can be completely honest about this, so thanks for that. Anyway, my ex, Charlie, wanted to give it another go. She cheated on me the first time around, so I was hesitant, but I think she's really changed. I *hope* so, at least "

Isa was incredibly relieved, and she just sat there and listened as Ming continued to tell her about Charlie. "She's amazing— very strong, very smart…not that you aren't either, of course, but…anyway. It seems like we've both made our choice. You still want to do that pizza and movie thing? Platonically?"

"Sounds good, Ming. Maybe we could even be friends."

"I'd like that," Ming said, "but…I think that tonight should be it, considering we've had dalliances in the bedroom area of things."

"Yeah, you're probably right,"

So they ate pizza and watched the documentary, and both of them swore and yelled at the TV screen. It wasn't exactly the most romantic choice for a date movie, which made it good that this had changed from being a date to just being two women who liked each other okay spending time together.

Ming left around ten, and she kissed Isa on the lips, one last time, before she walked out the front door of the apartment. "Stay cool, kiddo."

"You, too."

Isa grinned as she shut the door behind her. She knew she had made the right choice…but would Lilith think she had? Did she even want Isa to make this choice? Isa didn't have any way to know, not yet, but hopefully, the answer would come to her in that night's dreams.

She didn't dream of Lilith that night, though, and woke in the morning with an empty feeling inside. Where had Lilith been? Why hadn't she dreamt of her? Isa wanted to tell her how she felt, but without her entering Isa's dreams, she couldn't get the message to Lilith—the message that she loved her, and that she wanted her, and that she was the one Isa had chosen.

Which reminded Isa, yet again, of how crazy the idea of spending the rest of your life with someone like Lilith was. Isa couldn't touch her, couldn't kiss her, unless she was asleep. She knew she wanted Lilith, knew it was almost like she *needed* Lilith, but was that enough?

She spent the rest of the day wondering if it was, and then she decided to call the only person who could understand her predicament—Iriana. She invited Isa over for dinner, and Isa picked up a nice bottle of red wine on the way there, as it seemed what she had to ask Iriana about would be helped by drinking.

Iriana had prepared some lasagna and garlic bread, as well as a Caprese salad, with fresh basil and fresh mozzarella, about which she said, "The only way to make it is with the freshest ingredients possible. Otherwise, it's practically inedible."

As the meal progressed, Isa began to think that she might have been a little more generous with each of her own pours of wine than usual, and Iriana seemed to notice this. "Something troubling you, Isabelle?"

"Yes, yes. Very much so. How…how did you make up your mind about your dream woman?"

"About Aileen?" Iriana took another sip of wine, another bite of salad, seeming as if she wanted some time to think it over. She finished chewing, then said, "It was obvious, I suppose. Just fucking obvious. You must know what that's like, with your dream girl. That is, if the obviousness of your feelings for her has made itself known by now."

"Oh, has it ever!" Isa sighed, and took another swig of wine.

"We should discuss this, then, and we should also have you sleep over on my couch. You're a bit too…sloshed to go home. And it's getting late."

"Thank you. All of that is a good idea. A great one. And yeah, I'm a little…woozy. Drunk, maybe. Yes, drunk." Isa reached for her wine glass again, to swallow the very last drops of the wine, then knocked it over. "Oh shit."

"It's fine, dear, it's fine…only a few drops of wine on an already heavily stained table." Iriana mopped up the little spill with her napkin, then leaned back on the couch. "So, how are things with Ming?"

"There are no more things with Ming. She's…she has someone she likes now, just like me, only her someone is…real."

"Oh, and your dream girl, she isn't real?"

"She's not…here. On earth. In my arms, in my bed. Nothing like that at all. And it sucks!" Isa collapsed onto the back of the couch, suddenly feeling quite spent.

"Yes, I certainly know how such a situation can…suck, as you put it. Do I ever! But be grateful that you still have her, dear. Enjoy her. As I'm sure she enjoys you."

"But I'm *not* sure of that! I don't know how she feels. I mean, I *think* she likes me…loves me, maybe. She's given me gifts, lovely ones. But the last dream…God, who knows what she was thinking in that one."

"Well, my dear, why don't you sleep on it? Perhaps she'll come to you tonight. Perhaps all your answers will come to you tonight, too. But I have to get up early tomorrow. I'm going to a gallery to talk to the owner about a possible show of my art. I've…I've started painting something else."

Isa hadn't even taken the time to ask her about her art. To ask her about her anything, actually. Which made it seem important, now, to do just that. "What…what are you painting instead of her?"

"My other dreams. I'll show you in the morning. But right now, it's time for both of us to get some sleep. I'll get you some sheets and a pillow."

Iriana left the room for a few moments, then came back in and made up the couch for Isa. The way Iriana was taking care of her made Isa think of her mom. Iriana seemed somewhat like Isa's mother—yes, just a little. They certainly had their differences, Isa thought, but they also had the same subtle gentleness, and Iriana spoke a little—just a little—like her mom had. Isa's mom had called her "dear" just like Iriana, and Isa's mom's voice had held the same notes of care and love when she called her "dear."

Isa felt the subtle ache that always came with thoughts of her mom, thoughts which got in the way of falling asleep. And for once, she didn't fall asleep thinking about Lilith. Well, not exactly. Some of her thoughts did contain Lilith, and the one Isa had closest to falling asleep was a moment of wondering if her mom would have liked her. Yes, Isa decided, certainly. Because how could anyone not? She smiled at the thought, and soon enough, she was fast asleep.

CHAPTER TWENTY-THREE

Lilith had decided not to enter Isabelle's dreams that following night; she needed to put some distance between them. But that quickly proved to be impossible. Yes, there was physical distance between her and Isa, and yes, she wasn't going anywhere close to Isa's dreams, but her head was full of thoughts of Isabelle. Was she with Ming right then? Was Isa thinking of her, by any chance, the way she was thinking of Isa? *Did* Isa think of her when they weren't together? And, most importantly, did Isa feel the same way about her as she felt about Isa?

Lilith couldn't stop focusing on Isabelle, so she did what usually worked when she was in this state—she masturbated. But of course, that certainly didn't manage to pull her thoughts away from Isa. No, touching herself concentrated said thoughts on Isa even more, because her fantasy self wanted what her real self wanted—Isabelle, in her arms.

In her fantasy, she and Isabelle were lying on a bed, which sat in the middle of a grove of trees. The dappled sunlight looked beautiful on Isabelle's bare skin, the light and dark playing across her flesh in a most magical, beautiful way. And soon, Lilith's fingers were playing across Isabelle's skin, too, a dance of delicate touches, the slightest brush of skin against skin. But she knew that, however light her touches were, they still were turning Isa on, because Isa was moaning, arching, pushing back against her hand. So what could Lilith do but move her fingers farther down, down to where Isabelle's pleasure spot lay, down to her clit, the same fingers that had danced across her flesh now dancing across her most sensitive of areas.

Lilith teased Isabelle for a while, her touch still gentle, delicate, then a hint of more pressure…and then less, not even close to enough to get Isabelle off. And then, in her fantasy, Isabelle said, "Please," and what could Lilith do but comply? She added more pressure, centered on Isabelle's clit, pushing, circling, not teasing any more. No, now her touch had one purpose and one purpose alone—to get Isabelle to come.

And she did, only a little while later. Isa arched her back and came, came hard.

And Lilith came hard, too. But afterward, she felt emptier than before, because being in Isabelle's dreams was much better than Isabelle only being in Lilith's fantasies. Better, but still…not good enough. Not by far. No, she had to see Isabelle, Isa herself, and she had to use the only way that really mattered. She had to come to Isa in her dreams.

But would that be a bad idea? Aileen had warned her about having her powers taken away, and the fact that what she was doing wasn't allowed…well, that worried her. The wounded look in Aileen's eyes when she spoke of her lost love, the love whom she hadn't seen in years…well, that worried Lilith even more. To have Isabelle ripped out of her life, that was a pain she could not bear. And certainly not for the rest of her life. So she would have to keep this under wraps. She would have to hide her visits to Isabelle somehow.

That night, when almost everyone else was at their mirror, Lilith sneaked into her own room in the hall of mirrors, the one that held her own mirror. But she couldn't visit Isabelle there any more, or she might be caught. So she used a spell on the mirror, a spell all Dreammakers knew, and the mirror shrunk to the size of an apple. Lilith placed it under her cape and sneaked herself and her mirror back to her house, where she grew the mirror back to its actual size. Before she'd left her room in the hall of mirrors, she'd taken the time to place a dummy mirror on the wall where her real mirror had hung until then. It wouldn't fool anyone for very long, but she'd only put it there as an afterthought. It was there just to trick the casual glance, the only kind their mirrors ever got from the higher-up Dreammakers.

With the mirror now placed in a dark corner of her bedroom, Lilith prepared to wait for nightfall in Isabelle's city and to slip into Isabelle's dreams once again.

But she couldn't handle just sitting there and waiting. Impatience grew in her, stronger and stronger, and so she got out her bowl, filled it with water and magic, and looked down at Isabelle, who was wandering around a large apartment at the moment.

The apartment seemed to be filled with paintings, sculptures, too, and they all appeared to feature the same woman, each one of a woman with the same hair and the same body. Then Lilith looked away from Isabelle and saw a woman entering the room, possibly coming in from outside.

The woman was gorgeous, if a little old for Lilith, but she could see the woman still had a startling amount of beauty in her face. She was graceful too, as she bent down, placing some coffee and a bag on the table in front of Isabelle.

"Here," the woman said, "I got us some sustenance. Bagels and lox. Cream cheese, too. And, since I know you like them so much, two mochas. I never liked them much myself, but they seem to be growing on me." The woman looked sad, Lilith realized, with an air of...loss, was it? Yes, with an air of loss surrounding her.

"Thanks," Isabelle said, smiling at the woman. Oh, what a beautiful smile, Lilith thought, wishing desperately that the smile had been directed at her. Maybe, this night, it would be, if she was lucky.

"I know it's a little late in the day for breakfast, but I didn't want to wake you when I went out to the gallery to talk to the owner. He's a real character, turns out. Part of the family."

"The...family?" Isabelle asked.

"Yeah, you know, part of the queer family. It's a phrase some of us use. I guess...you're pretty new to all of this, aren't you?" the woman said.

"Well...yeah. I started having those dreams, you know, about that woman, and they kind of opened up my eyes to who I think I really am." "Dreams"? "That woman"? Was she talking about Lilith? She had to be! So she *did* think about Lilith when they weren't together in her dreams. But why was this woman allowed to know about the dreams? And did she...no, she couldn't possibly know they were real.

"My dream woman opened up my eyes as well. I had only dated men up until then, and she showed me who *I* really was." This woman had a dream woman as well? Could she be...no, it couldn't possibly be the case.

"When I met her for the first time, well, when we had *sex* for the first time, I should say...she basically had me instantly," the woman continued, as she began removing what looked to be food from the paper bag. "I accepted being gay that first night, and I've never looked back. Besides, men never really held my interest in the first place. Especially in the bedroom."

The two women chuckled, and then Isabelle said, "I have to say, looking back, I did enjoy sex with men, but all those times, none of them hold a candle to my times with a woman." With a woman? So she *had* slept with Ming. An eruption of jealousy flashed across Lilith's skin. This woman—Ming—had gotten to touch her in real life. Something Lilith would never have. She started regretting eavesdropping on Isabelle, but what Isabelle said next completely changed her mind.

"And I hope this isn't TMI, but with Lilith, it's so much better than it ever was with Ming. No offense intended toward her. But Lilith…well, she really, *really* knows what she's doing. Her touch is like…wow, it's just…yeah, wow!"

The woman grinned, a very wicked, suggestive grin, and cocked one eyebrow. "Well, don't even get me started on my times with my dream gal. Fireworks, young lady, fi-er-works."

"But, you know," Isabelle said, a smile fading from her face, "she's only in my dreams. I can't touch her."

Yes, Lilith thought, and that's not enough for you, not for someone as special as you are. You deserve…better than that.

But before Lilith could convince herself to stop watching them, Isabelle spoke again, and what she said convinced Lilith to keep watching, at least for a little while longer.

"What you said, though, about fireworks…that's not all there was to your time with Aileen, really. It wasn't all, was it?"

Lilith leapt up, almost knocking the bowl off the table. Aileen? *Her* Aileen? Was this woman…was she…?

And then Lilith's question was answered.

"I'm right, Iriana, aren't I?" Isabelle said in a gentle voice.

"No, Aileen, she was obviously, definitely, *certainly* so very much more than just sex." Iriana collapsed back onto the couch with a sigh. "Oh, I'd give anything to have her back, just once. Just one more time, just to know why she disappeared. I mean, I'm trying to get over her, I really, really am, but it's…it's fucking impossible!"

"I'm sorry," Isabelle said, and she gently placed her hand on Iriana's shoulder.

"I'm sorry, too," Lilith said. "I will do everything I can to bring you that one last night. I promise." She knew the woman couldn't hear her, knew her words didn't hold as much power as she wished, but yes—she would do everything she could to bring Iriana and Aileen back together. Because Iriana looked too sad, and Lilith was certain that Iriana's time with Aileen had been just as special as her time had been with Isabelle. Now, if she only knew how—how to lead her friend back through a mirror and straight into Iriana's dreams. There had to be a way, and she would give all she had to find it.

But right now, she finally had to admit to herself that she and Isabelle weren't the same. They didn't live in the same world, and they couldn't be together, not in the way Isabelle wanted, or in the way she deserved. And Lilith knew she would choose Ming in the end, because who in their right mind wouldn't? Ming might not have been the woman of her dreams, but Lilith was only the woman *in* her dreams, and that was far—very, very far—from enough.

CHAPTER TWENTY-FOUR

Isa thought that it was very kind of Iriana to let her spend the night, and to bring her breakfast—which was more like lunch, actually—just when Isa was starting to get hungry. She'd decided by now that Iriana was an especially lovely woman, and Isa just wished she could bring her and her dream woman, Aileen, back together. Maybe Lilith has a way, Isa thought as she sipped her mocha.

"So, what are your plans today?" Iriana asked. It was certainly about time they stopped talking about their dream women. It was too painful a topic for either of them to talk about it any longer.

"I don't really know. I mean, I need to do some writing, but maybe I should work in a nap. You know, to see if Lilith will show up. I miss her, I guess. Yeah, I miss her." Isa swallowed the last bit of her mocha, then stood up. "Thank you so much—for letting me spend the night, for the mochas, and for being the only person on earth to think my story isn't completely crazy."

"Well, perhaps I'm not the only person, but I'm guessing that the others might be hard to find, to track down. I'm almost certain that there are others like us, others whose loves come to them in dreams. Oh, boy, does that ever sound corny!" Iriana grinned at Isa, and then her smile fell a bit. Isa felt incredibly guilty, a feeling that made her realize that she just *had* to find a way to reunite Iriana and Aileen. But how?

"Yes," Isa told Iriana as she got ready to leave, "I think a nap is in order. Although I don't know if I'll be able to sleep, considering how…desperately I want to see Lilith."

"Hmm, maybe some chamomile tea?" Iriana followed her to the door, enveloping her in a lovely hug right as she reached it. "Take care of yourself, dear, and enjoy your time with Lilith. If only I had known to…well, if wishes were horses. You take care. Good-bye."

Isa got back to her apartment in the early afternoon, and while she needed to do some writing, it was the last thing in the world she wanted to do. All of her thoughts were on Lilith, every single one of them *about* Lilith. Every single one.

So she made a cup of chamomile tea with five teabags in it, hoping that overdosing would do the trick. And after downing the dregs of the tea, she barely had enough energy left to make it to her couch, collapsing onto the cushions with the last bit of her reserves.

Soon, she was fast asleep. And yes, Lilith, thank all that was holy, was there.

❖

This time, Isa was walking toward a beautiful, ivy-covered cottage in the middle of the woods. The path was raised and made of pale bamboo, and the section that was about four feet away from the house sat above a small, quickly moving stream the color of tropical waters, a rich, clear aquamarine.

Isa knew she didn't need to knock before entering the cabin, so she just pushed the door open and went inside. The room, with large windows, held only a bed and a kitchen table to the left, with four chairs, and then, farther to the left, Isa noticed all the necessary kitchen appliances: stove, fridge, and a large, marble-topped counter.

But those things barely mattered to her, because on the bed, wearing nothing but a smile, was Lilith.

Her hair was in a thick, shiny braid, hanging over her right shoulder and blocking her right breast. Isa wanted to reveal that breast, take the nipple into her mouth, suck on it until Lilith couldn't take it anymore…but, no, something had to come first.

"Lilith…before we…before I…what I mean is that we need to talk about something."

"And what would that be?" Lilith's voice could best be described as a purr, pure sex and sensuality, but with a slight undercurrent of fear, and her face was tight, her lips tense.

"It's just that…I…I've loved our time together, and—"

"And now it has to end, is that it?" Lilith's face fell, no longer impassive. It now showed her fear loud and clear. "I suppose you've decided the smart thing—if you can't have me in the real world, this dream world I come to you in, it's just not enough. Is it." And those last two words were not a question at all. "You've chosen Ming, and wisely so. I don't blame you in the least."

And before Isa could say anything or, especially, say the most important thing—that she loved her—Lilith was suddenly in front of her, kissing her, and seconds later, and so very suddenly, Isa was coming, coming, coming. And then…

❖

And then Isa woke up, still in a sleepy haze, suddenly full of the fear that she'd never see Lilith again. Lilith seemed to think that they were best apart, although her response to Isa, to the words she thought Isa was going to say, well, that told Isa everything she needed to know. Lilith loved her, loved her deeply, just as deeply as Isa loved her back. But she hadn't given Isa the chance to tell her if the love was returned, instead blindly jumping to the conclusion that Isa had chosen Ming over her, that Isa had chosen the real world over Lilith's dream one.

And so, heavy with sleepiness, and even heavier with sadness, Isa dragged herself into her bedroom, even though it was still light out. She crawled under the covers and was soon fast asleep again. Isa dreamt of nothing for hours, but when she dreamt again, her dreams were not kind, and there was no Lilith. No, instead, her nightmare man was back, and this dream of him, this nightmare, was worse than all the others combined.

Chapter Twenty-five

Lilith stepped out of the mirror in tears, but her bedroom was not empty when she entered it. In front of her stood three men, two other Dreammakers named Perry and Garth, and Francisco. All had angry expressions, but Francisco looked downright furious.

"We have been watching you, Lilith, and I am very sorry to say this, but you must be stripped of your powers. Tonight. You know that you are not supposed to grow attached to humans, you know this, and yet you still..." Francisco raised his hand to the bridge of his nose and pinched it, wincing. "You don't know how sad this makes me, but we must do this. You are not meant to do what you have done."

He reached for her, but Lilith was quicker than him. She leapt back through the mirror and back into Isabelle's dreams.

"Damn it all!" Francisco yelled. Then he lowered his voice, looking from Perry to Garth. "What can—is there any way, any way at all for us to get her out?"

The other two men, who had been anxious the entire walk there, each shook his head.

Perry was the first to speak. "No, Francisco. It is impossible for any of us to enter another Dreammaker's mirror. They're tailored especially for each of us, and no one else can use them."

"Except—" Garth said.

"Yes?" Francisco barked, narrowing his eyes at Garth.

"Except for our current queen. And Amaya. They have more power than any of us, especially the queen. Perhaps she could find a way to enter the mirror."

"Perry, go to her at once. See if she has a way. And hurry!"

Perry didn't hesitate for a second. He took off running, out the open door of Lilith's house, dashing toward the hall of mirrors. He arrived there about ten minutes later, gasping for breath, but he rested for only a few moments, then went straight to the mirror for Rebecca's palace.

Arriving through the palace's mirror a little bit later, he rushed straight to the bottom of its stairs. At their top, he didn't bother to knock, but just threw open the front doors. He loudly yelled, "Rebecca?" as soon as he was inside.

No one answered, and none of the servants were there to answer him, either. So he ran to the room where Rebecca was most likely to be—the library, which connected to the hall of records. When he got to the room, Rebecca was sitting there in one of her large, flowery armchairs, deep in what looked to be one of the more recent record books—or, possibly, something else? At that moment, though, it didn't really matter.

Rebecca's head jerked up as soon as Perry entered the room. "Perry," she said, her voice quiet. "What brings you here?"

"I have come from our village. There has been a problem."

"Yes? And what is it?"

"Lilith—she's fallen for a human and has stolen her mirror and sneaked it into her home. And now…now she has gone through the mirror, and we have no way to get her back out, no way to take away her powers as we are supposed to do."

"Then I suppose I should join you and travel back there. Besides, I hear that your leader has still not returned, which worries me. Is Francisco currently in charge?"

"Yes, Queen, he is. We should…we should hurry!"

"I agree," Rebecca said, her voice full of something Perry couldn't quite place. It almost sounded like there was something else, some other reason for them to hurry. Had she discovered something in the record books?

She shut the book she held, then slipped something into her skirt pocket. "Shall we?"

"Yes, Queen."

They took off down the hallway, and Rebecca surprised Perry by going faster and faster, until she was running. A servant stood at the front door this time, and he barely had time to open it, as Rebecca and Perry gained speed, racing toward the castle's mirrors to all the villages. Rebecca leapt through the one that led to the village Perry had come from, and moments later they arrived in that village's hall of mirrors. Rebecca, because of her great power, was able to travel faster through the mirrors than any other Dreammaker, and she'd used some of her power to bring Perry along with her at the same immense speed.

"Now," Rebecca said, her chest heaving a little, "where does Lilith live?"

"Follow me," Perry said, and they picked up speed again, arriving at Lilith's house just a little while later. A crowd had gathered around the house, and Rebecca had to push her way through at first, until the Dreammakers began to recognize her. Then, they parted quickly, letting her pass through them with ease. Some fell down to one knee, but Rebecca barely noticed.

She was here for one thing alone, and it was certainly not because Lilith had entered her mirror, it was certainly not because she had fallen in love with a human. No, it was because she had fallen in love with the *wrong* human. The same human that the nightmare creature had been trapped inside of. The one whose mind he might be able to escape from, if given the chance. And quite possibly, that chance would be given soon—very soon—

because of the power that Lilith had been feeding him by her many visits to the woman's dreams.

Rebecca knew that Lilith had more power than any average Dreammaker as soon as she reached the mirror. A wave of Lilith's energy hit her as soon as she came within a few feet of her mirror. It was putting off a glow, too, a sign that Rebecca had hoped would not be there, a sign which told her that if they didn't stop the power in time, the nightmare creature would escape. And if he did, it would take only hours before the whole human city lay in ruins. So Rebecca certainly did not have much time.

The nightmare creature, as Rebecca had learned from Cillian's journal—which had been hidden in a drawer in their library—had been created by the power of the many nightmares the Nightmaremakers had brought to the people of the woman's city. The cumulative force of all the nightmares had built him into a real thing, traveling from one dream to the next, but they had managed to trap him in the woman's head the night she was born. Cillian had been in charge of the entrapment, but why he had kept it hidden from her, she didn't know. Well, she would have plenty of time to find that out—plenty of time, as long as she succeeded.

The paper she had placed in her pocket was old—very old. It had some confusing words on it, words that seemed to be about containing the nightmare creature—containing him or, possibly, destroying him. It said something about building up power and sending it through the mirror. Rebecca had an idea about how the power could be built up, but what about the last line on the paper? That was the most confusing part of the words. There, it simply said, "A shared blessing shall save them all."

She had no idea what that meant. But it was critical that she figure it out, because that was where the page ended, with those seven words. What on earth could they mean?

CHAPTER TWENTY-SIX

L ilith was waiting for Isabelle. She was back at the cabin where her heart had been broken, and she most certainly did not want to be there. But she had no choice. It was either here or a life without bringing anyone dreams, a life empty of a single chance more to see her love. She was startled to find that she was crying, something that had happened to her only a few times before. Humans cried all the time, she knew, but she was not very familiar with the feeling. It was awful, those wet, runny tears sliding down your cheeks, the quiet sobs that made your chest heave a little—that made *her* chest heave a little now. No, she did not like crying. Crying out in ecstasy, that was one thing, but this, to use human slang, flat-out sucked.

And now it was going to get worse, because the door to the cabin was opening—Isabelle was here now. And it was time to be reminded, yet again, that Lilith's love was not something that could ever be returned.

But when the door opened, it wasn't Isabelle who stood there. Instead of her, a black, flickering figure stood in the doorway, large and horrible, with a wide, sharp-toothed grin.

"Will Isabelle be here soon?" he growled, his voice sending goose bumps racing across Lilith's skin. "I'm ready to be free now, silly little Lilith."

He took a step closer to her, and she couldn't help it—she screamed. She tried to exit the dream, but all she could do was change it.

Now, she was walking in a meadow. It was a dark night, with only a few stars and a little moonlight to guide her. She saw Isabelle in front of her, only a few feet ahead, but as Lilith walked toward Isa, she never got any closer to her. Soon she was running, because she heard footsteps behind her, whispering across the grass. And finally, she caught up to Isabelle, grabbing her hand and starting to pull her along. "We've got to hurry!" Lilith said, her voice sharp but quiet. "Follow me!"

Isabelle turned to her and froze, almost knocking Lilith over. "I know. I know we have to hurry, but he'll catch us eventually. He's never caught me before, but this time…this time I know it's different." Tears were running down Isabelle's face, a face empty of all color.

"I know you're scared, but there's got to be a way. I just know we can find it. But we've got to hurry, sweetheart, or we won't have time to find the solution. Please, please, darling."

At that final word, a small smile flickered across Isabelle's face.

And so they took off, and Lilith ripped a hole through the dream, doing her best to sew it up tight behind them, although she worried that he'd still find a way through.

Now they were in a crowded marketplace, somewhere foreign. Sharp, spicy, enticing smells met their nostrils, and the stalls around them were filled with strange fruits and bright, loud-colored fabric.

"It's beautiful here," Isabelle said, taking in the scene around her.

"We're in India. I'm guessing it will be hard for him to follow us here, because it's so unfamiliar. I suspected that you'd never dreamed of India before, and especially not an Indian marketplace."

"I think you're right. And let's hope you're right about the monster not finding us here." Isabelle looked a little less afraid now, possibly, and her face had gained a little color. Which was good...although it could have just been from the running. And they would probably—definitely—not be safe for long.

"I don't think we've gotten away from him forever, Isabelle. We should keep moving. He might still be able to follow us here. In fact, I'm certain he'll be able to. So, come along now, quickly, darling." Lilith just barely noticed Isabelle smile again when she finished her sentence. What had she said to cause that reaction? Why was Isabelle smiling so often, in a time when so much terror must be flowing through her? Well, there would be plenty of time to sort such things out later—if they survived.

And then Lilith began to wonder about other things, too. Were they the only ones threatened by this creature? Or did he hold power over others as well? But, she reminded herself, they had plenty of time for questions *later*. Now, they just had to stay safe. Now, they just had to stay alive. People could obviously die in dreams, and if the dream was powerful enough, their real bodies could die, too. So Lilith began pulling Isabelle along once more. They passed stall after stall, the people parting just in time for them to get past, and the two of them knew better than to slow their pace. Lilith did her best to send energy from her own power straight to Isabelle, but the only kind of power she had to give was sexual, so a flush came to Isabelle's cheeks, her chest as well, and even at a time like this, Lilith still got pleasure from affecting Isabelle that way.

"You're doing dirty things to me, aren't you, Lilith?" Isabelle asked as they half-walked, half-ran past the stalls.

"It's the only way I know to keep you going. You know, sex gives you energy—at least, my kind of sex does."

"Does it ever!" Isabelle grinned.

And then her grin disappeared, because now they could both hear the creature's razor-sharp terror of a voice behind them, and he sounded like he was close, and was quickly getting closer—and would soon be *too* close. "Please," his voice came, only a few steps behind. "Please, I only want to be free! I only want what is mine, what the nasty Dreammakers stole from me! Shae wants me to be free, too, you know!" His voice became sharper, angrier as he continued to call out across the crowd, across the shrinking distance between them. "Shae knows what's right…the other Dreammakers are sick in the head! But you don't have to be, Lil-ith," he whined. "You can do what's right, and *free* me!"

"Shae?" Lilith gasped. *Shae wanted him to be free?* How could a fellow Dreammaker want to free something like *that*? What were her intentions? More importantly, though—was he even telling the truth?

"Who's Shae?" Isabelle seemed frozen in place, but at least her mind was still working well enough for her to ask the important questions. And that one certainly was important. Who *was* Shae, if what the creature said was true? Was she no longer a friend of the Dreammakers, but now an enemy? There would be time in just a bit to figure that out, if only they could get away to where they needed to go—the safest place in all of Isabelle's dreams, and the place where Lilith held the most power.

"Never mind Shae. I'll tell you at the next location we go to. We should have some time once we get there. But, right now, you have to run. As do I. Come on!" She grasped Isabelle's hand once more, and they took off, toward the tear Lilith was creating in the dream. Only one thing would hold him off, because she was starting to think about where he might have come from, after his mention of Shae, the current queen of Isabelle's city's Nightmaremakers. But had Shae created him, or had something else? Well, they could figure that out later.

Right now, running was the only thing to do, and so she and Isabelle ran, as fast as they could, the nightmare creature behind them, slipping through the market stalls and people like a shadow, or a ghost. Nothing seemed to stand in his way. Worse, even, was that her every glance backward showed he had grown a little bigger. And even worse was the fact that each quick glance backward also showed he had gotten closer. So they ran on, through the marketplace, till they reached a tall, wide brick wall, almost crashing into it.

"But…how…" Isabelle stammered, shaking a little.

"Don't worry, I still control your dreams. He doesn't have enough power yet." Lilith began to pull at a crack in the brick wall, and only then did Isabelle finally realize Lilith was naked, had been naked the entire time.

"Funny thing, I just noticed that you aren't wearing anything. I guess…I'm a little distracted." Isabelle's voice shook as she spoke, but at least she was still herself, Lilith was relieved to realize. The nightmare creature hadn't broken her yet.

Lilith was beginning to crack under the pressure, though, so she made the hole in the wall quickly and rather sloppily. Hopefully it would still work. Soon, she had fashioned a hole big enough for each of them to fit through the wall—a tight fit, but it would have to do. They ducked through it and then Lilith put the pieces she had pulled apart back together, smoothing down the edges with her hands. Now it looked as though the wall had never had a hole in it, or even a crack.

"Hopefully that will hold him. Now, we're almost there, we're almost there." Lilith was doing her best to soothe her friend—were they friends?—or whatever the right word for Isabelle was. Yet again, something to worry about much, much later. But they had reached their destination, and for now, at least, they were safe.

In front of them rose the large mansion where they had first met, where they had first fucked, where Lilith had first begun to find the woman who stood behind her interesting. Now she was far more than interesting, and now, Lilith was going to try the only way she knew to conquer the nightmare creature. She would use the only power she had, the place where her strength all flowed from. She was going to give Isabelle the best sex of her life, even if turned out to be the last thing she ever did. Because, was there ever a better note to go out on than one of mind-blowing pleasure?

CHAPTER TWENTY-SEVEN

Rebecca had watched everything unfold in the mirror. She'd watched the nightmare man arrive at the cabin where Lilith had gone, watched the nightmare man chase Lilith and Isabelle through the field and through the marketplace, and watched him start following them to the mansion where they had apparently first "met."

Of all the people possible, all the ones whom she brought dreams to, Lilith just *had* to choose this woman to fall in love with, this woman who happened to house one of the most dangerous creatures known to the Dreammakers, a creature that could destroy the human world in just a number of days. He couldn't be let out. And he couldn't remain in Isabelle's dreams any more, either, a ticking time bomb just waiting to explode out of her dreams and into the real world. All he would have to do was catch her and kill her dream being—just that one simple thing in order to free himself. Why he hadn't accomplished this yet was a mixture of Dreammaker power and Isabelle's own strength and goodness as a human being. Cillian—who had decided to keep this secret from her for some unknown reason—had certainly chosen the right woman to trap the creature in. Now, if only she could remain the right choice for just the next few minutes.

It was time, Rebecca decided, as she watched Lilith lead Isabelle into the mansion, into a room filled with warm light and not much else. It was time to begin. She and Lilith's village of Dreammakers could certainly help, potentially a large amount, but Lilith and Isabelle would have to solve the last part of the puzzle—"A shared blessing shall save them all"—on their own, because Rebecca didn't have the slightest idea what it meant.

She lifted the mirror and started walking toward the house's front door, carrying it through the rooms. The Dreammakers who'd been in the cabin with her followed her outside. She set the mirror down on the ground with relief and a soft grunt. The mirrors were heavier than they looked when they were attached to the walls where they belonged.

"Everyone!" Rebecca's voice rang out over the crowd, and upon hearing it, all the Dreammakers fell silent. "I have something to ask of you all. In order for this creature to not be released, we need to send all the power we can into the mirror. We need to have what humans call an 'orgy.'"

Several Dreammakers gasped, but in delight: almost all of them seemed not to be offended in the least. After all, sex was what they did, and they did it *well*.

"Those of you who wish to abstain, you are more than welcome to leave and return to your homes. I would suggest that you masturbate once there, and send as much of that energy back here as you can. Those of you who are partnered, please find your partner among the crowd. Those who are not, find someone eager and willing. That shouldn't be very hard for any of you, I would assume."

She was rewarded with deep and knowing laughs in response to that last sentence. Most of the crowd was smiling, some were grinning, and those who weren't were beginning to scan the crowd to look for willing—and eager—partners. Many of the Dreammakers were already in relationships, duos, trios, or more, and Rebecca watched as each grouping formed. Soon enough, almost everyone was kissing, groping, and pleasuring each other. She noted with a smile that not a single Dreammaker had left. Well, except for one. An older woman with red-and-silver hair had quietly departed from the crowd, with a sad expression. Rebecca would have to find her later, to learn what her story was, and why she was the only one to leave.

"Good, good, everyone! Now," Rebecca said, pausing as she scanned the lovely crowd of half- and entirely naked Dreammakers. "Now, send as much sexual energy as you can toward the mirror. And if someone would be willing to be *my* partner, I think I can contribute a hell of a lot of firepower!"

Only seconds later, a woman and a man approached her. Both were already naked, and both were beautiful. The man had shoulder-length, curly blond hair, the loveliness of it bringing the word "mane" to Rebecca's mind. He had a delicate but strong build and a not-so-delicate, sizable hard-on pointed right at her. The woman was lovely as well, with straight, black hair flowing all the way down her back, and her full breasts and hard nipples seemed to be beckoning to Rebecca's salivating mouth. She hadn't made an agreement with Cillian that this would be allowed, but the fact that this was required to save lives would temper any hurt feelings. Besides, she'd been in a threesome with him many years ago…twice. Maybe a third time with an especially gorgeous woman would help ease the ache this would cause.

But none of that mattered now, because among moans and cries of pleasure, the woman and man began to kiss her and disrobe her, the woman sucking on her earlobe and then her neck as the man unzipped her dress to her hips and then dropped it, the soft velvet caressing her hips and legs as it fell to pool around her ankles. She hadn't been with a woman in a while, and really, she realized, as the man began to kiss her, she needed female energy to send into the mirror. "I'm sorry," she said softly, turning to the man, "I'm sorry, my dear, but I think, for Lilith's and Isabelle's sakes, and for everyone else's…I think it's best if I have sex only with a woman."

The man looked a little disappointed, but he merely stated, "Yes, Queen, as you say," and shortly, a man of equal attractiveness had swept him into his arms, and moments later the two men were entwined like long-separated and now-reunited lovers.

"Now," Rebecca said, turning toward the woman and wrapping her arms around her, "what do you like best? What things can I do to your lovely body to bring you the most pleasure?"

"I like to have my ass fingered while someone finger-fucks my pussy."

"I think I can manage that." Rebecca led her to the field where everyone else was fucking, making love, or both. She lay the woman down on the grass and spread her thighs, delighted to see that she was already soaking wet. "You get aroused fast, don't you?" Rebecca said, staring at the woman's swollen labia and hard clitoris.

"Oh, yes, Queen, it only takes me moments to get this wet."

"You don't have to call me Queen, you know. Rebecca will do." She spread the woman's pussy, then paused. "I'd be more comfortable if I knew your name before I started fucking you. It only seems polite."

"Claire, Que…Rebecca. It's Claire. Oh, God!"

Rebecca had barely waited until the woman—Claire—had finished introducing herself. Now that she had the woman's name, it was time to get down to business. A business that Rebecca seemed to be a natural at, judging by the way the woman was writhing around just from a few flicks of her tongue. Rebecca moaned against Claire's cunt, which only seemed to drive the woman even wilder, and so, just to take things up a notch,

Rebecca flipped around and mounted Claire's face. Claire took the hint instantly and got right to work licking her way up and down Rebecca's slit, bringing more moans from Rebecca.

"So," Rebecca said, her voice stuttering and thick, "you like getting both your holes fucked at the same time, do you? What a dirty, dirty girl." She kept her cunt on the woman's mouth and praised the Dreammakers' creator for the fact that their torsos were just the right length for her to eat Claire out as Claire ate *her* out. Now, though, it was time to do what Claire had requested, and so she sucked on a few of her fingers and then leaned down, arching her back, and began to circle Claire's asshole, which seemed to do the trick. Claire's moan rose to a shriek as Rebecca slowly pushed her fingers into Claire's ass and pussy at the same time, and soon Claire was coming, screaming, her sounds vibrating against Rebecca's cunt, and yet the lovely young lady still didn't stop eating her out. Soon enough, Rebecca was coming, too. It didn't manage to top her orgasms with Cillian, she was glad to discover, but fuck if it wasn't a good one.

She collected as much of the sexual energy from her orgasm as she could, sending it straight toward the mirror, and now she could feel the magic from all the sex singing through the air, all of it traveling at lightning speed toward the mirror.

But inside the mirror, a quite different scene was playing out.

CHAPTER TWENTY-EIGHT

"Are we safe now?" Isa asked Lilith. Although she was almost certain they weren't, she still had high hopes, despite the utter and complete terror she was feeling—high hopes that this would end well. Even though she knew better, even though she felt the truth in her bones. The truth that they obviously *weren't* safe now, and beyond that, that Lilith might not love her. Which one was more important? It would seem like her survival would be top of the list, but, well…

"For now, for now we are. And now…now I have to ask you to do something. Something that should help keep us safe for a while longer." Lilith gestured toward the bed.

"Oh. Ohhhh. Okay, can't say I'm not game. I mean, I'm fucking terrified, but I've really got nothing better to do at the moment." Isa laughed, but her voice was high-pitched and shaky.

"Shall we, then, darling?"

"I love it when you call me that," Isa told her, taking Lilith's hand as she led Isa to the bed. She took in Lilith's beautiful naked body, the one she wanted so desperately to touch, the one she wanted to make love to her—the one that belonged to the woman she wanted *to* love her. "I'm ready," she told Lilith, who then pulled her into her arms and moved her lips to Isa's. They joined in a kiss that spoke of power, of fire, of passion. Then, quick as anything, Lilith tossed her to the bed and ripped her clothes off, leaving them in shreds.

Lilith kissed her again, then lay down on top of her, shoving her legs apart. She began to play with Isa's clit as she nibbled on her lips and licked her neck. Then Lilith's teeth clamped down on her shoulder, and Isa bit her lip—hard—to stop herself from screaming. It wouldn't have been a *bad* scream, but one of pleasure, because Isa was quickly realizing even more about what turned her on. Apparently she really, really liked being bitten, for one.

Lilith loosened her teeth from her shoulder a few moments later, and Isa sighed at the release of them, her body now flooded with energy, awakening from Lilith's bite and her touch. She was wet, she was ready, and she knew Lilith had noticed, because Lilith pushed up and then pushed in, sliding a finger, then two, inside her, one hand beginning to fuck her while Lilith's finger still flicked at Isa's clit. The sudden feeling of Lilith's fingers sliding in and out of her hole brought a moan from her, and the sensation of those fingers was like nothing she'd ever experienced before. Her whole body was alive now, tingles of pleasure dancing, arcing across her flesh, and she wasn't surprised to see little flickers of blue electricity sparking off her skin. The sparks spread to Lilith's, soon, because Isa had slipped a few fingers inside her as well, and now Lilith was moaning, too, writhing around just like Isa.

Isa took her free arm and rolled them over. Now she was on top, and she told Lilith in a voice that didn't sound quite like her own (because she had never said anything like it before), "I want to make you fucking come, Lilith. I want to make you fucking come…and come…over and over. Because I think if you come instead of me, the power will be greater."

"You're probably…oh, God…right about that, darling, but why don't we aim for both of us? At the same time?"

"Works for me," she told Lilith, and so they fucked each other, their hands dancing across each other's bodies, their fingers sliding in and out of holes that just got wetter and wetter. Isa kept her eyes open, watching the blue flickers grow, until they were crackling audibly, a sound not too unlike the sounds they were both making, strangely enough. As she continued to fuck Lilith and rub her clit—and as Lilith continued to fuck her and rub her clit—the flickers of blue grew bigger, and bigger still, grew along with their moans, with their arousal, until the flickers rose at least a foot into the air.

"More," Lilith moaned. "Oh, God, more…more!" What could Isa do but satisfy her request? And so she slipped a third finger into Lilith, and then a fourth, and Isa grew fuller as Lilith did the same. And then their thumbs went in, too, and Isa had never been that full before, and she told Lilith so.

"Good, good, but more, please, Isa, more." So she pushed in farther, up past her knuckles, until in went her hand, and now she was fisting Lilith—her hand slipping inside Lilith like nothing, like she didn't even have to try, because, God, was Lilith ever wet. And then, just as suddenly, her entire hand was inside Isa, and if Isa had thought she felt full before, well, this went beyond even that. And oh, oh, it felt *so…fucking…good*!

Their fingers kept at it too, as they fisted each other, and she could tell from Lilith's quivering underneath her that she was close. Isa, too, was so, so close, and then she heard a voice behind her.

"No, no! Stop!" It was the nightmare creature. "You've got to stop! Stop and free me! No! Nooo!"

But Isa knew she didn't have to listen to him. No, what she had to do was come, and so she did, Lilith, too, their cries echoing through the building. Their sounds were bouncing off the walls, going *through* the walls, and the electricity was flickering, and flashing, throughout the entire building, too. Because nothing—

nothing—had ever felt like this before. The pleasure might break her body, and Isa knew it had to be freed, so she let it pour out of herself with every sound she made, let it wash over every dream she'd ever had.

Especially every one she'd ever had about him—about the nightmare creature. Because he was screaming too, but they were not sounds of pleasure like hers, or like Lilith's. No, his time was ending, and his power was fading, just as hers was growing.

The building was trembling now, but Lilith slowly pushed her up. "He's not dead yet," she said, her voice weak. And Isa turned, and Lilith was right. He was walking toward the bed, scraping his sharp, claw-like hands against each other with a horrible screeching sound. And he was grinning, wider than ever, looking absolutely certain that he'd won.

"I don't—I don't know what else to do," Isa gasped. "I thought—"

"You thought...wrong..." came his voice, as he pushed himself up to his full height. "You can't stop me now. You tried. You failed!"

He had almost reached the bed now, and she watched as he raised his hand, pulling it back, getting ready to strike.

She had to say something to Lilith before she lost the ability to say anything at all. "I love you, Lilith," she whispered, turning to her, and Isa now had tears in her eyes.

"You do?" Lilith sounded shocked, but not unhappy, even though she had tears in her eyes as well.

"Yes." And just then his claws dug in to Isa, tore into her skin.

"I love you too, darling. I love you, too."

She heard a loud noise, then—*too* loud. She screamed as it crashed through her body.

Was she dying? Was that what it meant? Was that what someone heard when death took them to the other side? She didn't know, and so she did all she knew to do. She clung to Lilith as tightly as she could. She knew it was the right thing to do, somehow, even though she didn't know how, exactly, she knew that.

Then a bright, blinding flash erupted throughout the room, until she couldn't see anything at all, save Lilith. And then... nothing.

CHAPTER TWENTY-NINE

It was quiet where Isa was now…at least, quieter than where she had been. Something about this space felt familiar, although she was still in so much shock she couldn't manage to figure out why. She only knew she felt safe.

Lilith loved her. That was her first real thought. At least she hadn't died without finding out. The second thought was about where she was right now. Could this be…Heaven?

She slowly opened her eyes. Nope, not Heaven, unless Heaven had a bed with her sheets on it, and a bedside table holding some very brown flowers in a very fancy vase.

Her apartment. She was back in her apartment. Well, the vase and flowers aside, it all had to have been just a very strange dream.

But her bed felt weird. Soft, supple, and fleshy.

"Could you get off me, maybe, darling?"

She certainly could. Isa leapt up. Now she was very much awake, and certainly in the present. "What the…what the fucking hell?" she yelped. Because a woman lay in her bed. A naked woman. A woman with brilliant, garnet-colored hair, golden eyes, and a quiet, knowing smile.

"Li…Lilith? It was all…real? And you're…you're here?" She couldn't help it. She burst into tears. "Oh, God. Oh…God. You're real. You're real!" She pulled Lilith into her arms.

"I'm glad to be here too, darling, but you're crushing me."

"Oh. Yes, sorry about that." She loosened her arms, pulling back to stare at her, at Lilith…at the woman she loved.

"Did you mean what you said in the dream?" Isa looked down for a moment. Waiting for her answer terrified her almost as much as the dream had. But she had to know. "Did…"

"Yes, I did." Lilith smiled now, a gentle smile—the kind of smile someone gives to the one she loves. "Did you, then?"

"I think you know the answer to that, but…yes. Yes!"

She couldn't keep her hands off Lilith now. She had to have her, had to have her in the real world. And so she pulled Lilith to her once more and kissed her, hard, letting Lilith know her intent.

But Lilith pulled back from her, seeming strangely hesitant. "You should know that I've, um, never done this in real life before. I don't know if…if I'll know what to do."

"Oh, I'm certain you'll do just fine," she told Lilith, and she climbed onto the bed and straddled Lilith.

She was right. Oh, was she *ever* right.

They spent practically the entire next day in bed, just making love, with only a few bathroom breaks and meals. Lilith loved the human food Isa introduced her to, especially macaroni and cheese.

"This stuff is divine!" Lilith mumbled through a large mouthful. "I would almost give up sex for this stuff." She cocked an eyebrow at Lilith. "No, no, don't worry, darling. I'm not serious. Not with the kind of sex *we* have!"

"Just wait until you try mochas. Then you might actually consider it."

"Mochas, hmmm? We'll have to go out and get some soon."

"Sure, right after I fuck you again."

But the first things they went out and got, after groceries, were rings. The rings were silver, with opals embedded all the way around them.

Isa had begun to wonder what Lilith would do for work, considering she would use her main skill only around her. But when they got back from buying the rings, they discovered a large box in her bathroom, looking almost as if it had come out of the mirror. It was filled with precious jewels and gold coins, and a card lay inside of it, buried underneath all the immensely valuable things.

"Read it," she told Lilith, handing it to her, because it had Lilith's name on it. She did, and she chuckled when she seemed to reach the end.

"Here." And Lilith handed it to her, grinning.

Lilith,

Here are your thanks—and Isabelle's, as well. Your proclamations of love for each other apparently destroyed the nightmare creature. You may be wondering where he came from, so I will tell you. The darkness and power from all the nightmares the Nightmaremakers brought to Isabelle's city formed him. But Shae of said Nightmaremakers had learned of the nightmare creature and tried to work out a deal with him to gain power for herself. She arranged for me to be trapped in dreams until she could figure out a way to use my power to free him, but she failed, thanks to both of you. We now have her imprisoned, and she will pay dearly for her crimes. I hope both of you will be happy together for many years to come. Oh, and Lilith? You're fired.

Yours,
Amaya

"Fired, huh?" she said to Lilith, placing the card on the sink.

"Yes, they take away the powers of Dreammakers who fall for humans. Like my friend Aileen. Poor woman."

"Aileen? As in Iriana's Aileen?" She couldn't help but be a little shocked. So Lilith knew her friend's lost love. "Could there...could there be a way for us to bring them together?"

She noticed that Lilith was staring at the back of the card, and she watched as Lilith began to smile softly.

"I think they already *are* together, sweetheart."

Isa turned toward the card and noticed for the first time the writing on the back of it. She leaned forward a little and read what it said.

P.S. Lilith, we thought that you could use a familiar face. Get in touch with Isabelle's friend Iriana when you need a break from making love.

"You don't think..."

"Yes," Lilith said, her smile growing wider and wider. "Yes, I most certainly *do* think. Let's pay your friend Iriana a visit."

They did just that (after making love one more time), but upon their arrival, it wasn't only Iriana who stood there once she answered Isa's knock. No, she had her arm draped around a woman with red hair, hair streaked with silver, but hair that Isa certainly recognized. After all, she'd seen it from dozens of different angles and practically knew it by heart. The silver was new, though, but so was the woman's face. She had almost never seen someone look happier, but she was still surprised when the woman pulled her close for a hug, then slowly let go, kissing her on the cheek.

"Thank you," the woman said softly, then turned toward Lilith. "I thought I might see you here, too. At least, I hoped I would."

"Come in now, both of you, come in!" Iriana gestured her and Lilith into the apartment. She almost appeared happier than Aileen, and Isa glanced from face to face, then watched as Iriana placed her arm back around Aileen.

"And thank you, both, so very much," Iriana said, her voice lowering. But she wasn't looking at her, or Lilith, when she said it. No, she was staring into Aileen's eyes now, her face aglow, and Isa saw the same expression on Lilith's face. Yes, all three women's faces held the glowing smile that you only gave to someone you loved—the one whom you loved more than anything.

Then Isa followed Iriana's eyes to Aileen's face, and Aileen's face was the same as she thought her own must be whenever she stared into Lilith's eyes. Absolute, pure, undiluted love flowed from Aileen and Iriana. Love like she felt for Lilith. Love like Lilith felt for her.

"Yes," Aileen said, soft as anything, as she gazed into Iriana's eyes. "Thank you."

About the Author

Maggie Morton's erotic short fiction has been published in a variety of anthologies. Her interests include psychology, Buddhism, river otters (according to her partner, her totem animal), and delicious food. Her reading encompasses biography and memoir as well as speculative fiction and in particular, novels written about mysterious books. She lives in Northern California with her partner and their Japanese Bobtail.

Books Available From Bold Strokes Books

Month of Sundays by Yolanda Wallace. Love doesn't always happen overnight; sometimes it takes a month of Sundays. (978-1-60282-739-4)

Jacob's War by C.P. Rowlands. ATF Special Agent Allison Jacob's task force is in the middle of an all-out war, from the streets to the boardrooms of America. Small business owner Katie Blackburn is the latest victim who accidentally breaks it wide open but may break AJ's heart at the same time. (978-1-60282-740-0)

The Pyramid Waltz by Barbara Ann Wright. Princess Katya Nar Umbriel wants a perfect romance, but her Fiendish nature and duties to the crown mean she can never tell the truth-until she meets Starbride, a woman who gets to the heart of every secret, even if it will be the death of her. (978-1-60282-741-7)

The Secret of Othello by Sam Cameron. Florida teen detectives Steven and Denny risk their lives to search for a sunken NASA satellite-but under the waves, no one can hear you scream… (978-1-60282-742-4)

Dreaming of Her by Maggie Morton. Isa has begun to dream of the most amazing woman—a woman named Lilith with a gorgeous face, an amazing body, and the ability to turn Isa on like no other. But Lilith is just a dream…isn't she? (978-1-60282-847-6)

Andy Squared by Jennifer Lavoie. Andrew never thought anyone could come between him and his twin sister, Andrea… until Ryder rode into town. (978-1-60282-743-1)

Finding Bluefield by Elan Barnehama. Set in the backdrop of Virginia and New York and spanning the years 1960-1982, Finding Bluefield chronicles the lives of Nicky Stewart, Barbara Philips, and their son, Paul, as they struggle to define themselves as a family. (978-1-60282-744-8)

The Jetsetters by David-Matthew Barnes. As rock band The Jetsetters skyrocket from obscurity to super stardom, Justin Holt, a lonely barista, and Diego Delgado, the band's guitarist, fight with everything they have to stay together, despite the chaos and fame. (978-1-60282-745-5)

Strange Bedfellows by Rob Byrnes. Partners in life and crime, Grant Lambert and Chase LaMarca, are hired to make a politician's compromising photo disappear, but what should be an easy job quickly spins out of control. (978-1-60282-746-2)

Speed Demons by Gun Brooke. When NASCAR star Evangeline Marshall returns to the race track after a close brush with death, will famous photographer Blythe Pierce document her triumph and reciprocate her love—or will they succumb to their respective demons and fail? (978-1-60282-678-6)

Summoning Shadows: A Rosso Lussuria Vampire Novel by Winter Pennington. The Rosso Lussuria vampires face enemies both old and new, and to prevail they must call on even more strange alliances, unite as a clan, and draw on every weapon within their reach—but with a clan of vampires, that's easier said than done. (978-1-60282-679-3)

Sometime Yesterday by Yvonne Heidt. When Natalie Chambers learns her Victorian house is haunted by a pair of lovers and a Dark Man, can she and her lover Van Easton solve the mystery that will set the ghosts free and banish the evil presence in the house? Or will they have to run to survive as well? (978-1-60282-680-9)

Into the Flames by Mel Bossa. In order to save one of his patients, psychiatrist Jamie Scarborough will have to confront his own monsters—including those he unknowingly helped create. (978-1-60282-681-6)

Coming Attractions: Author's Edition by Bobbi Marolt. For Helen Townsend, chasing turns to caring, and caring turns to loving, but will love take five steps back and turn to leaving? (978-1-60282-732-5)

OMGqueer, edited by Radclyffe and Katherine E. Lynch. Through stories imagined and told by youth across America, this anthology provides a snapshot of queerness at the dawn of the new millennium. (978-1-60282-682-3)

Oath of Honor by Radclyffe. A First Responders novel. First do no harm...First Physician of the United States Wes Masters discovers that being the president's doctor demands more than brains and personal sacrifice—especially when politics is the order of the day. (978-1-60282-671-7)

A Question of Ghosts by Cate Culpepper. Becca Healy hopes Dr. Joanne Call can help her learn if her mother really committed suicide—but she's not sure she can handle her mother's ghost, a decades-old mystery, and lusting after the difficult Dr. Call without some serious chocolate consumption. (978-1-60282-672-4)

The Night Off by Meghan O'Brien. When Emily Parker pays for a taboo role-playing fantasy encounter from the Xtreme Encounters escort agency, she expects to surrender control—but never imagines losing her heart to dangerous butch Nat Swayne. (978-1-60282-673-1)

Sara by Greg Herren. A mysterious and beautiful new student at Southern Heights High School stirs things up when students start dying. (978-1-60282-674-8)

Fontana by Joshua Martino. Fame, obsession, and vengeance collide in a novel that asks: What if America's greatest hero was gay? (978-1-60282-675-5)

Lemon Reef by Robin Silverman. What would you risk for the memory of your first love? When Jenna Ross learns her high school love Del Soto died on Lemon Reef, she refuses to accept the medical examiner's report of a death from natural causes and risks everything to find the truth. (978-1-60282-676-2)

The Dirty Diner: Gay Erotica on the Menu, edited by Jerry L. Wheeler. Gay erotica set in restaurants, featuring food, sex, and men—could you really ask for anything more? (978-1-60282-677-9)

Sweat: Gay Jock Erotica by Todd Gregory. Sizzling tales of smoking hot sex with the athletic studs everyone fantasizes about. (978-1-60282-669-4)